I0576140

THE SPANISH BEAUTY

Elaine C. Wolfe

Lost Legends Publishing, llc
Anderson, Indiana,USA
7.5.606.5342
https://www.lostlegendspublishing.us/

Cover Art and Design by Marain's Studio
http://mariansstudio.us/

Printed in the United States of America.

ISBN: (print) 978-1-7339617-4-5
ISBN: (digital) 978-1-7339617-5-2

THE SPANISH BEAUTY

Elaine C. Wolfe

This book is dedicated to my son, Scott; my daughter, Leah; my daughter-in law, Audra; my son-in-law, Ricardo; and my three grandchildren, Cole, Tessa, and Joseba. This book would never have been possible without their support and love.

DISCLAIMERS

Please excuse me for taking liberties with the Spanish police, court, and punishment systems; train schedules and routes through three countries; the non-use of some of the accented Spanish vowels and the ñ in some of the words which I used; and the realignment of the topography around the city of Toledo, Spain. All these changes made for easier writing of the story and plot lines.

Many of the Spanish names given characters in this book were based upon my Spanish friends whom I know or have known. Some of the names will have special significance to some of you. Please excuse me if I've offended anyone, it was purely unintentional. The Spanish way of name-giving by genealogy makes more sense than our American way. And, the Spanish language is beautiful when spoken well. I'm still trying to learn it myself. Please excuse that I've given Margarita the last name Elliot, which wouldn't necessarily occur in Spain. Many married women in Spain might never take their husband's last name or might, but hyphenate it with their own last name.

ACKNOWLEDGEMENTS

First, I wish to acknowledge my parents who always encouraged me to read and learn. They didn't have the opportunity to go to college during the Depression years, but they were determined that I would be able to have that luxury.

Second, I wish to acknowledge the many colleges and universities, especially Purdue University, in preparing me to be an award-winning science educator.

Third, I wish to acknowledge my children, Leah and Scott, for proof-reading this book chapter by chapter. Their suggestions and corrections enabled me to finally reach one of my life-long ambitions, to write a novel.

Fourth, I wish to acknowledge my grandchildren, for wanting me to finish this book and saying "Grandma, you have to finish it because I want to read it".

Fifth, I wish to acknowledge my friends, both artist and teacher ones, who were anxious to read what I was working on and to encouraged me.

Sixth, I wish to acknowledge all my wonderful students over the years. They made my life full of joy and satisfaction. When I saw the "lights go on in their eyes", I knew why I had chosen the teaching profession as my life's work. Many of them have continued to stay in touch over decades and become some of my close and dear friends.

Seventh, I wish to acknowledge my friend, Marian Betts, as a fellow Indiana Wildlife Artist, author, and CEO of Lost Legends Publishing, LLC, who pushed me to write and publish this book. She told me "if I can, you can." She also created the artwork and designed the cover.

Lastly and primarily, I wish to acknowledge God who in his mercy has granted me a long life, good health, good family, good friends, and so many innumerable blessings that I can't mention them all here.

CHAPTER 1

THE COMMISSION

CHAPTER 1

THE COMMISSION

It had been the same since Medieval times. The blade sharpener's whistling song from his Pan Pipes echoed through the narrow streets of the village calling the inhabitants whose scissors or knives needed attention. I sat in my attic studio and listened to the changing pitch of the whistle as the grinder's path wandered up and down the barrio streets. Lower pitch and volume as he moved away and higher pitch and volume as he came nearer. I had to hurry to get to the villa and my next sitting scheduled for this morning. Never had I worked so hard as on this particular commission and I had never wanted to do a more spectacular job as with this one. I grabbed my coat and my purse and practically ran out the door, bumping into the grinder as he passed my apartment.

When I reached the villa and looked at the amount of work that I had accomplished and contemplated the amount of work yet to be done, I became worried. There was still so much to be done. The canvas before me had taken hours of preparation. I was just finishing the beginning stages of the painting - doing the many preliminary sketches, studying which ones would be best to include, deciding on which pigments to get the required hues, choosing the proper brush strokes to obtain the wanted textures, doing a perspective analysis, blocking in the initial colors, and the furtive first brush strokes. The painting had reached the stage of ugliness. What many patrons don't realize is that all paintings go through an ugliness stage on the way to being even partly finished. Sometimes paintings have to go through several ugliness stages before even approaching a finished, and hopefully, a masterpiece stage. I was sure this painting wouldn't be finished for weeks, but at least I was on schedule, a schedule that required it to be done and accomplished on time.

When one accepts a commission, the possibility of failure is always present, but the rewards and success can be great. Such is the life of being an artist. The trials and the tribulations are always present, sometimes more so and sometimes less. Not many commissions had come my way since moving into this new village. I had only lived here for eight months. In order to take on commissions, one has to usually establish oneself in a community, build a reputation, and only then can an artist finally garner a share of the local patronage. This painting had the potential of giving me a shoo-in into the local painting commissions and sales or of permanently blocking my chances of future income of the local art revenue. All my expertise would be used to make this canvas special, special for its patron and special for me.

I had drawn since the time that I could hold a pencil at three. Doing artwork was like eating, breathing, and sleeping to me. It was part of my soul. I couldn't remember a time when I hadn't been making artwork. The years of lessons had flown by and working in a variety of media had progressed in the same manner as with most artists, especially the old masters. I had worked first in pencil and charcoal, then in pastels. I had progressed to oils and watercolors. Even printmaking had offered years of experience. Subject matter had also progressed from doing still life drawings, to landscapes, and finally to portraits of animals and humans. Step by step my career as an artist had developed. All seemed to go well until my allergy to turpentine and mineral spirits had eventually caused me to switch from oils to acrylics. After having learned the techniques of painting and the theory of color mixing pigments in oils, the switch continued unimpeded. Only the medium had changed for me. Most people who saw my artworks thought that I still worked in oils. My acrylics were not garish or too bright as with many artists using acrylics. It was fortunate for me that people couldn't tell the difference between my oils and acrylics because I could command the same prices for my acrylic paintings as I had when my artworks were in oils. My colors reflected the more subdued tones and hues of nature's own colors. I loved to paint landscapes and seascapes and in my last village, where I had moved after a long apprenticeship, I had been well-known for these landscape and seascape paintings. While I had sold fairly well, there were too many artists in that vicinity to really make an income which didn't border on the "starving artist" livelihood. My mother had always desired that I not become an artist. Her comment of "you can't make a living as an artist" dogged my every footstep as I tried valiantly to prove her wrong.

This painting would not be my normal artwork, but I had been approached with an offer that I couldn't refuse. Late one afternoon I had been sitting at an outdoor café sketching the setting and the patrons. Streaks of sunlight were slanted through the plane trees overhead and produced dappled patterns of light on the tables, patrons, and pavement. The sky was a beautiful shade of azure and added to the shadows' deepness and sharpness. It was the perfect lighting to a tranquil scene that had spoken to my soul and artistic heart. The café was fairly busy, but many of the occupants in the outdoor area were staying for several hours, talking and laughing together. I felt very much alive and wanted the ambiance to last forever. Having completed a couple of quick sketches, I was determined to try to do a much more detailed study of those who were staying over longer drinks and tapas. One couple who was engrossed in conversation became the object of this longer study and sketch. I placed the waiter next to their table in the sketch as though he was delivering their drinks and entering into their conversation. As I continued drawing, I must have been totally absorbed in capturing the moment. I hadn't seen Señor Elliot until he approached my table. He must have stood there for several minutes watching me. Perhaps he had been there longer than I realized watching my efforts in capturing the people, the table, their food, their drinks, and their personalities.

His first words to me was to introduce himself stating,

Chapter 1 - The Commission

"My name is Charles Elliot and I have been watching you several minutes now. I particularly like what you have done in your sketch here", as he pointed down to my unfinished sketch. "You've not only captured the likenesses of the couple and the waiter, but you have caught their personalities, gestures, and body language."

I was flabbergasted because I not only had been unaware of his watching me, but I was amazed that he could have thought that I had done the scene justice. I stammered, "Hello, my name is Marielena Cortez. It's nice to make your acquaintance. Thank you for your compliments".

He answered, "It is a pleasure to meet you. I don't think I've seen you here before. Do you come here and sketch often?"

"Not often but today is such a beautiful day, and the light is just right", I answered.

"Do you live here in the village?"

"Yes, I just moved here eight months ago. I moved from Rhonda."

"I have been looking for an artist to do a commission for me. My wife will be celebrating her twenty-eighth birthday within the next six weeks. I would like it if you would paint her portrait for the special birthday celebration that I have planned. The portrait would also be part of the gift which I will give her."

"I usually don't accept portrait commissions. I could recommend a fellow artist whose specialty is portraiture", I replied.

"Whether or not you usually do portraits, I think your talents and abilities would do nicely for the job", he said pointing to the sketch again. "You could nicely display just the right ambiance that I'm looking for. And, I think, you could capture my wife's personality in this commission. I would very much like you to consider my offer."

"I really don't feel that I could take on the job."

"Please reconsider and take the job", he answered.

I thought for a moment and, not wishing to be rude, but

also not wanting to accept the commission, I quoted him a figure for doing the commission which I considered astronomical. I also stated, "If I accept the commission half of this amount will have to be paid up front and will not be refundable. The remaining half will be paid upon completion of the painting if you approve of the painting. If you don't approve of the painting, the painting will become my property to be disposed of as I see fit. All of these conditions will have to be in writing so that both you and I understand the terms of the agreement." From prior experience with the few commissions which I had done in my past, I realized that I needed to protect myself in any arrangements of this type. I had not made these agreements once before and had found myself unable to defend myself when a patron had not liked the painting which I had done for them. I had almost not been able to pay my rent or eat because I hadn't protected myself. Experience is a very good teacher.

The amount which I had quoted him was so high that I assumed that he wouldn't want me to do the commission. Also, with the stipulations, most patrons, unless they are very serious, wouldn't comply. To my surprise, his response was, "Done!" He hadn't even taken time to seriously consider what he was agreeing to, but immediately had accepted. How could I argue with that? He must seriously want me to do this commission.

Evidently, I had somehow quoted him a figure that he was not only willing to pay, but which he could afford. Whether I had wanted the commission or not, now I had it.

The next hour and a half sped by quickly as we continued to discuss the size, colors, and composition of the portrait. What was the date that he foresaw my completion of the project? How could I get the contract to him for our signatures? Where could I have the pleasure of his wife's company to begin preliminary sketches? What was her name? How should she be dressed? Was this to be a formal portrait or more casual? What kind of background would be required?

The portrait would be formal. "I will give you more

instructions on the size and composition when we meet later as I'm still working on that. Perhaps you'll be able to help in that regard. The background will be a room in my home with a combination of still life, with objects inside the room, and landscape, with the outside gardens showing their beautiful flowers. And my wife's name is Margarita."

It seemed to me that he had already thought a lot about this commission before deciding on who should do it. It seemed that choosing an artist to paint this portrait had actually been somewhat of a last-minute decision for him. Was it chance that had brought him my way on this particular day? Why me? Maybe good fortune was smiling on me in this new village? Who knew? But I wasn't about to argue at this point.

"You can bring the contract with you when you begin the painting in my home", he said. Then he quickly wrote me the check covering the down payment of fifty percent right then and there. He obviously had no problem with paying the other half upon completion of the project.

Other information which we exchanged that day included how we could contact each other with telephone numbers, addresses, and full names. It seemed to be a situation which I hadn't wanted, but was stuck with.

CHAPTER 2

POOR LITTLE RICH BOY

CHAPTER 2

POOR LITTLE RICH BOY

Sir Charles Elliot, "Lord Elliot", had always gotten what he wanted. As a child he threw temper tantrums whenever he didn't get his way. As an only child, he had been indulged by both of his parents. They had been told by the doctors that they could never have any more children, so they put all their hopes, dreams, and efforts into Charles. The Elliot family was extremely wealthy. Both parents had inherited billions from their parents. Going back three generations both families had been and remained landed, titled, and industrious with their feet planted firmly in aristocracy and royal friendships. They had wealthy business associates and relied on many close-knit banking franchises. Their home was a Tudor mansion on a prominent hilltop in southern England within easy commute to London via train. This enabled Charles's father to have a business within close distance which helped him run the far-flung family empire. Banking, railroads, marine shipping, petroleum, electricity, and later airlines kept the family fingers in almost all areas of the globe when England had controlled the finances of the world and England had colonies to exploit worldwide.

Charles's grandfather and his father were interested in research and development - and they later managed to pass these interests on to Charles. The family's business holdings had been expanded by them so that as England and the world had changed since the First and Second World Wars, the Elliot family holdings had basically remained unchanged throughout the years. With a little tweaking here and there, some shrewd business dealings, and many hours of cultivating the "right people", the overall holdings had remained relatively consistent in percentages of the gross national product of England as a country.

Chapter 2 - Poor Little Rich Boy

Even though, Charles's father, the Lord Edward Elliot, was a healthy and robust man with flaming auburn hair, grey-blue eyes, and a florid complexion, he was prone to drink in excess, particularly whenever fox or wild boar hunting. He could upon occasion become a mean-tempered drunk who took his feelings of superiority out on anyone who came near him - wife, son, servants, or business partners. He was noted to be quite arrogant and refused to be corrected. He failed to see that he might possibly be wrong once in a while.

Charles's mother, Lady Anne Elliot, was a strikingly beautiful blond, slender of frame, pale in complexion, and placid of temperament. She loved her husband dearly and was unaware of his many infidelities. She trusted him implicitly and always took his word whenever he said that the business empire, which he had inherited and ran on a "24-7-365" basis required him to stay in London many nights or required his many business trips to Madrid, Berlin, Rome, Milan, Jakarta, Manila, Venice, Paris, and other major cities in India, Burma, Japan, and Australia. When his father was on these long business trips, his mother was left in control of running the household, bringing up Charles, and attending social functions as required by their family status.

Charles's grandmother, Lady Elizabeth, was in poor health and her health was deteriorating even more as she continued to age. Charles's grandfather had passed away several years prior and so Lady Elizabeth lived alone. Lady Anne, Charles's mother, sometimes went to see to her mother-in-law's doctors' appointments and hospitalizations. Lady Anne's parents had also passed away so that her mother-in-law was all she had left by way of parents. During the times when Lady Anne was with Lady Elizabeth, Charles was left alone ... sometimes for days on end. Charles had a nanny, and later governess, named Alys, who also doted on him, letting him get away with almost anything, including letting him sleep with her. She also allowed him to run his hands all over her well-endowed body. As he became older, they became secret lovers with her instructing him in all the secrets of women's sexual arousals. Their trysts continued until he eventually left for college and he no longer needed a governess. Alys was always careful to teach him ways to prevent pregnancy so that Charles knew all about "the birds and the bees", long before most of the young men of his age knew of these matters. His mother had no idea that this was happening as she was entirely too busy with other matters.

When Charles was between the ages of 5 and 8, he had private tutors who came to the mansion and instructed him in English, French, and Latin. Special tutors were brought in for music, art, science, and math. When he reached preteen years, he was instructed also in history, government, and Italian. As teen years arrived, his family chose prestigious private schools, having their chauffeurs drive him daily, with the goal of grooming him to take over the family business. He added business studies to his already heavy list of subjects. He was quite bright and adapted nicely to whatever course was set before him.

With added years throughout his teens he knew that he could not rebel in terms of education, perhaps in other ways, but not education. He was smart enough to realize that to be successful in later life he would have need of the education which his parents were providing. But he chose to rebel in regard to his friends whom he always met outside his home. To please his parents' taste of activities and/or companions, both male and female, whom he brought home or pursued with his parents, especially at the country club, and which brought their blessings, were of the "proper breeding" to fit his and his parents' status. Early on Charles lead a double-life; what he wanted versus what his parents wanted. He became a wonderful liar, secretive and sly, a thief, and an all-around scoundrel. In the meantime, he always gave the impression of being a fine, upright member of society, and an outstanding citizen of the world with all the proper credentials, upbringing, and education. Speaking four languages fluently was as easy as being two different people.

Now whenever he wanted something, instead of throwing

childish temper tantrums, he adeptly used others, manipulating them to get whatever he wanted or making others do his bidding. Regardless, he still always got what he wanted. He knew in his heart that he was evil, but he had realized that he really didn't care. He cultivated the veneer of respectability with such aplomb that no one suspected his dual nature. When he had finally finished his formal education at Oxford and when his father had finally started to relinquish control of some of the family business to him, he was as ruthless in business as he was in his private life. He quickly learned German, Spanish, and Russian; and, therefore, he extended the business even further than his father had. And his father, not realizing the circumstances of his son's successes, was known to brag about his son's qualities and business acumen to friends, relatives, and acquaintances.

Because of his dealings with both sides of society, some of his business practices would have scandalized his father and his father's friends and business associates, but they never realized what he was up to. With much of the business now being beyond England's borders, he prevented his father from learning of these many less-than-kosher transactions. All his father knew, or really cared about, was that he was making money hand-over-fist and extending their holdings. To his father, Charles was a tremendous asset to the family.

In terms of Charles's love life, he never allowed himself to be trapped into marriage. Like in everything else, he was ruthless and took what he wanted. He sampled women, like a bee samples different kinds of flowers. He told himself that when the time came to marry, he would choose a woman who would make an excellent mother, who could be controlled, and who could satisfy all his needs. If for some reason, she ceased to fulfill all his sexual expectations, he could always resort to extramarital affairs to satisfy his tremendous appetites. After all, even though his father had always been able to hide his affairs from his mother, his father hadn't been able to hide them from Charles; and look at what a wonderful marriage his mother and father had. In the meantime, his wife would become the type of woman, like his mother, who stayed at home, took care of all the domestic matters, took care of all their children, and loved him enough never to question his comings and goings. Hopefully he could find such a woman who could meet all his qualifications. Until he could find such a woman, he was perfectly content and would continue with his bachelor life as he pleased.

Another consideration in choosing his future wife would be to satisfy his parents in deciding on a socially acceptable woman. It would never do to expose his dual-life to his parents. He needed to maintain his socially acceptable status, especially in marriage. His wife would need to be the proper "British Lady", be able to go to the opera, the country club, and to teas. She would have to have gone to the appropriate schools as well.

Because he had branched out in business, especially into Italy, and spoke fluent Italian, he came to the attention of the Mafia. While he was careful around the Mafia members, he made some very close friends of a couple members of the younger generation and worked with them to complete several business ventures requiring "muscle". One of his associates managed to seriously injure some family members of a banking colleague who had refused to extend a loan to Charles. Charles had applied for the loan in order to take over a small factory in Milan whose products were really much better than the Elliot family's products and were giving them too much competition. Charles considered the loan a small temporary fix to this much bigger problem. The loan would drive his competitors out of business and expand his control of the product, not only in Italy but in the overall European market. With the help of his young Mafia friends he was able to send a strong message to not only the competing factory owners but also to the banker. Several small factory explosions added impetus to his eventually getting the loan and his acquiring the competing factory. He had killed two birds with one stone, acquiring their business and manufacture as well as acquiring their product designs. As he had explained to his father by phone, he had been very lucky in business. Meanwhile, he was laughing at how he had again manipulated everything to his own benefit.

By the time Charles reached 36 years old, his parents had started insisting that he marry and continue the family dynasty by having children. While Charles was reluctant to give up his bachelor ways, he had slowly come to realize that he'd reached the point where he had to bow to his family's wishes and started hunting seriously for a wife. After all, his societal status would suffer if he procrastinated any longer.

TALE OF MARGARITA

CHAPTER 3

TALE OF MARGARITA

Margarita Ruiz Mendoza Serrano Nadal was born in Santanyi, Mallorca, Balearic Islands, Spain. Her beautiful dark eyes enchanted everyone including her parents. She was the youngest of six children born to an auto mechanic and his wife. Her parents had been young children (almost babies) during the Civil War and had married in their twenties. Her older brother had been born twenty years before her, during the years following World War II. Then her mother miscarried twice. The younger two boys and two girls were irregularly spaced so that by the time she arrived her siblings were 20, 14, 13, 10, 9, and 7 years old. She became the surprise and youngest child. Her mother, now becoming elderly, continued to work in the local grocery store as a cashier. Her siblings, with the exception of her older brother who worked with her father in the garage, were her playmates, babysitters, and nannies. With so much attention, she appeared much older and precocious. As she became older and her siblings all married or found jobs outside the home, she was now being left alone for days. She turned to her books, reading voraciously. In school she excelled in all subjects and truly loved learning. Her favorite teacher was her language arts teacher who taught her in her native Mallorquin - Catalan; Castellano - regular Spanish; and introduced her to English.

With the older children leaving home, the household had more money available for educating this youngest, favorite child. She was given piano and voice lessons. It was said that the neighbors paused in the street or in their nearby homes whenever she was singing or playing the piano as she was so talented.

By the time she reached her teenage years, she had caught the eye of the local talent agents, not only because of her music abilities, but also because of her great beauty. She won some local beauty pageants, becoming Miss Santanyi, Miss Manacor, and Miss Mallorca. She also gained the recognition of many local politicians who decided that, because no Balearic Island girl had ever become Miss Spain, they would finance her in hopes of sending her to the Miss World competition. Her less than affluent parents saw this as a chance for her to advance and become noticed in the world. In addition to that, maybe if she succeeded, they'd get more money for the entire family too. They encouraged her to accept the financial help, the tutoring, modeling lessons, and additional music lessons. At the age of 22 she won the Miss Spain competition to the delight of everyone in Mallorca, and advanced to the Miss World Competition which that particular year was being held in Milan, Italy.

Her patrons chose a gorgeous bright red silk gown for her talent competition and she chose the First Movement of Rachmaninoff's 3rd Piano Concerto for her talent. She had easily won the swimsuit competition in a strikingly beautiful silver and white suit that complimented her dark skin, hair, and eyes. She had a lovely hourglass figure that seemed meant to be looked at from every angle. During her musical performance, she wowed not only the judges, but took the breath away from the entire audience. At last as a finalist she reached the question and answer segment of the competition where she was competing against only four other contestants. During the final question and answer part of this competition, Margarita stood out with her response as to what she intended to do during her year reign as Miss World if she won.

"My heart and mind go out to the poor children of the world who have never had a chance to learn to read and who in many cases go to bed hungry at night. If I become Miss World, I would spend my year traveling to those areas of the world with funds from donors and my own winnings to bring food and learning to these unfortunate children. I would hire teachers and set up schools as well as set up food pantries." Her response brought a huge applause from the audience.

Margarita captivated the entire audience, but especially the young men, including Charles Elliot. Even though he was in attendance with several of his Italian businessmen and their wives, fiancées, or girlfriends, he had eyes only for Margarita. His date for the evening became incensed at his lack of attention to her and stormed out of the theater halfway through the evening.

After the competition, which Margarita won, there was a huge reception for all the participants and dignitaries. Charles made every attempt to meet this dazzling competitor. He felt that he would die if she weren't in his arms and he knew without a doubt that she just had to become his wife. She was what he wanted and wanted badly. Even though he knew nothing of her background, upbringing, dreams, aspirations, or future plans, she would be his and his alone. It wasn't as though he didn't always get what he wanted.

If an outsider could have compared their backgrounds, personalities, abilities, or life philosophies, he would have advised against the match as there were probably no two people as unsuitable for each other as these two.

Of course, during the next few weeks Charles put on his most charming manners, politeness, and gallantry, becoming the most ardent of suitors to this raven-haired beauty. For a man who was never turned down by any woman once he made up his mind to have her, Margarita really didn't have a chance to say, "No".

He sent her flowers, candy, and passionate love notes. He took her to the most expensive restaurants to wine and dine her. Through all these attentions Margarita continued to review her desire to help unfortunate children. Her wish was to fulfill her obligations to her supporters, to the citizens of Spain, and to her parents who had helped her advance to her goal of being Miss World. She had signed a contract when she won Miss World that committed her to a year of work. The monies which she had won renewed her wish to help her own family monetarily. Her family had always been so poor, but supportive of her, that her sense of thanksgiving to them was one of the strongest drives in her life to help them as they had helped her.

On the evening of his marriage proposal it was quite cold and blustery. He arrived to pick her up with a huge box in which there was a beautiful full-length black sable coat for her to wear to dinner. Looking at the coat finally triggered her overall response to him. Yes, she had been flattered by his attention, gifts, and overtures of love for her; but she was solidly grounded in her own world and wishes. She realized that Charles had never really tried to listen to her whenever she had tried to tell him about her hopes and plans. He said he loved her, but he hadn't really spent the time communicating with her. At first, she refused to wear the coat, but Charles prevailed, insisting that her own coat was inadequate for cold weather. She finally reluctantly agreed to put it on and wear it to dinner.

Charles had made reservations for them in the most expensive restaurant in Milan; and, as they entered, numerous diners recognizing Miss World requested her autograph. With every interruption Charles felt his patience and confidence waning. He had always been the one that everyone wanted to be with, wanted to have an association with, or wanted to have favors from. It was a little strange for him to now be playing second fiddle to someone else, even one as beautiful as his fantastically gorgeous girlfriend.

At last they sat alone in their secluded corner table. He had specifically requested a very isolated, romantic table with just the right combination of lights, flowers, and separation from other diners. The crystal, china, and silver gleamed on the table. The spotless white damask tablecloth emphasized the dazzling little lights over them. And Margarita looked positively radiant. Charles made a toast stating, "To your loveliness."

Margarita blushed and replied, "I know that you think I'm lovely, but look around. There are many beautiful women here. You should be toasting them, not me."

Charles was taken aback but decided to forge ahead. He

sweetly asked her, “What do you prefer on the menu?”

After considerable thought, she said, “The filet mignon”.

Charles decided to follow suit and also ordered the filet. He asked the waiter to bring a Spanish Rioja wine to compliment the beef. He also ordered this particular wine to align himself with this, his Spanish beauty, and her Spanish heritage. After their meal was served Margarita became increasingly quiet. So that when the last of the meal was finished and the waiter had cleared the dishes and had brought a bottle of champagne, she had said nothing at all for several minutes. Charles assumed that she was finally aware that he was going to ask her to marry him. In reality, Margarita was feeling sorry that she had allowed herself to be wooed when she knew she had other commitments that didn’t include Charles. She wasn’t sure how to tell him what was in her heart. As usual, their minds, hearts, and spirits were in different places with different agendas.

As the waiter left the champagne in the ice bucket and retreated from their table, Charles slid out of his seat and sank to his knees beside Margarita’s chair. He began his speech stating, “You must know how much I love you. Perhaps, therefore, it probably doesn’t come as much a surprise that I am now formally asking you to become my wife. Will you marry me?”

Margarita looked at him and stated very plainly, “No!” Continuing from that she said, “You really don’t know me, my family, my culture, nor MY plans. You have never inquired what I want. You’ve been under the impression that I would take you at face value. Never have you suggested that I meet your family. I have inquired into your background and, while it seems that your family is important to you, it seems that it doesn’t have the significance of my family to me. I therefore cannot accept your proposal. Furthermore, you seem to have forgotten that for this next year I am not my own person. As Miss World I have obligations which I intend to fulfill.” Standing abruptly, she headed for the exit, leaving Charles only the comfort of the discarded sable coat and the wasted champagne.

Chapter 3 - Tale of Margarita

Charles was dumbstruck. Always he had gotten what he wanted, and he had been so infatuated with her that he had wanted her. He reached into his pocket and threw money on the table which more than covered the bill, grabbed up the coat, and ran after her. He caught her just as she exited the establishment.

"I'm so sorry. I thought you had grown to love me too. Whatever you want, I'll help you succeed. I can't bear the thought of losing you. What must I do?"

As the next year flew by, he quickly realized that Margarita was indeed like his mother, being dedicated to her promises and responsibilities. She had made the contract to do some duties as Miss World and was determined to fulfill that contract. He became even more infatuated with her and swore to himself that he would indeed have her as his wife even if it meant that he'd have to forego other things. He contributed to her causes and sent her monies to cover her expenses.

But as the year went by, he started to have his same feelings and needs whenever he was on business trips. He thought that as long as he was free, he would indulge himself. He justified his actions by thinking she's doing her thing and I'm doing mine. To keep up appearances, he arranged his schedule to be with her whenever possible and at those times he showered her with flowers, gifts, jewelry, furs, and the best food and wines. He gave her the impression that while she was off being Miss World, he was languishing and pining for her; that his whole world was Miss World.

She started to feel guilty about not seeing him more. "Maybe I do love him - I certainly miss him when he isn't around". The moment came, her year was over, and she returned to Palma. He met her with flowers, and bending on one knee in the airport, he asked her again to marry him.

"Yes", she answered. And people in the airport applauded as they kissed.

Finally, he said, "I'm taking you home to England to meet my parents and I want to meet your family as well."

THE SPANISH BEAUTY

The next several weeks was later described by Margarita as a whirlwind romance with travels to her family for Charles to win her family. He even asked her father's permission to marry her in the age-old traditional way that won not only their permission but also their hearts. And, they traveled to England where this beautiful girl of his quickly won over his parents, especially his Lady Anne who hoped secretly that she would end her son's philandering. While Charles's father had always been able to hide his indiscretions from her, his son had not. His mother had over the years developed a number of suspicions, especially from overhearing some whispered gossip at the country club about her son's escapades and a few very specific warnings from a couple of close friends. She had tried to warn his father, but Lord Edward had only stated, "Boys will be boys". Now they would have a daughter-in-law who seemed both beautiful and wise and was young enough to give them grandsons - rightful heirs to their vast holdings. It seemed an ideal match. It mattered not one whit that she didn't come from English royalty or nobility, she was accomplished, educated, and cosmopolitan. No wonder Charles had fallen in love with her.

A lavish wedding on the Elliot family grounds saw hundreds of well-wishers. Charles flew in her entire family for the nuptials. He purchased a large villa outside Toledo, so she could at least live in Spain where she grew up, and close to Madrid, where he had multiple business dealings. Toledo and Madrid were tied by rail and plane to all the other family holdings so that commuting for him would be a breeze.

Perfection!

Charles had what he wanted. He'd had to wait a year for it, but now he could please his family with heirs; he had a wife who could raise a family; he had a beautiful home; and he had the business interests that would take him to cities with beautiful women from which he could continue to sample if things got boring. "Ah, what a life!" He said to himself.

CHAPTER 4
THE MARRIAGE

CHAPTER 4

THE MARRIAGE

Oh, married bliss! The newlyweds were extremely happy. Margarita felt that she was living in paradise. Never had she thought that she would live in such a wonderful house. Her husband was all smiles. He had at last gotten his fondest wish - a beautiful wife who doted on his every word and deed. Yes, the wait had been worth it. The only problem was that no matter how often or how hard they made love Margarita remained barren.

He had thought that her young age, plus his reputed sexual prowess, would surely enable them to have children. He assumed if they mated like rabbits, the results would end in an heir. But no. Months went by with increasing worry on both of their parts. He was sure it was her fault. She began to question his abilities. Stressful conversations evolved, even arguments, and even more forceful lovemaking resulted but with no baby. This couldn't be happening. They had been married almost two years and were still childless.

On top of that there were some black clouds on the horizon for his family's enterprises. He, as his father's health declined, was being required to travel almost every week to some other business venture all over the globe to "put out fires" that his underlings seemed unable to handle. Everything had seemed so easy when he had been a bachelor - his business acumen, his love life, and his ability to come and go as he pleased.

The pressures on him were starting to take a toll. He was drinking more, plus he had found the pleasures of cocaine. He made sure that he used it only as the pressures became too much on him - occasionally, not habitually. He realized that it could ruin him physically as well as mentally. Furthermore, cocaine and his business ventures wouldn't be mutually beneficial to anyone.

What he didn't realize was that it was also having an effect on his ability to perform in the bedroom.

As he hurried from their home in Spain to England, to India, to France, to Germany, and then back home again to Spain, he decided that they needed to find out why they couldn't conceive. Arriving home unexpectedly he discovered Margarita crying. Her eyes were bloodshot, her hands were trembling, and she was hunched over the table on the balcony where she had placed a huge cup of hot tea. He rushed to her side as she blurted out, "My period came again. It's as heavy as usual. Why can't I have a child? I so much want one!"

"My dearest, Margarita, I think we need to contact Dr. Rafael Mendoza in Madrid to have you evaluated. I've been researching the names of prominent OBGYN physicians in Spain and his name came up repeatedly as a marvelous doctor. Can I call and make an appointment for you?"

Very quietly and with a huge sob Margarita answered, "Yes - call him."

Because of Dr. Mendoza's busy schedule an appointment could not be arranged until two weeks later. Margarita was terrified and kept asking herself, "What will they find? What is wrong with me?"

The examination went smoothly. Her past history of heavy menses lasting from eight to nine days was noted, as well as a history of extremely painful menstrual cramping. The doctor finally said, "I think we'd like to have an MRI taken to be sure that structurally you are all right." Margarita was then issued the necessary forms to report to the hospital for that test and some other blood tests to check on her hormonal levels.

"How long will this take?" Margarita asked.

"Probably not over an hour at best for the MRI and only minutes for the blood work," was the doctor's reply. "But the results won't be known until several hours or a couple of days depending upon the number of patients being examined."

Indeed, it was not until two days later that the doctor called with the news that he wanted them to meet him at the office to view the MRI and to hear his findings. With trepidation they greeted the doctor as he asked them to take the seats across his desk from him.

"It is with a heavy heart that I'm sharing this MRI with you," he told them. He then switched on the light behind the MRI screen and pointed to a view of Margarita's uterus. "These," he said, pointing to a collection of ovoid objects with multiple tendrils on the MRI, "are fibroid tumors and your uterus is filled with them. They are the reason for your heavy flow and your cramping. They are also the reason that you haven't conceived since hormonally you are perfectly able to produce eggs. I came to my own judgements, but the reason I waited to make this appointment was that I wanted to consult with all the doctors on our staff. They concur that you will never be able to have a child."

The news was what they had both been afraid to hear.

"What do we do? Are these tumors removable? Can they shrink in time?" Charles asked.

"They are not removable, because they are too extensive. They will shrink, but not until Margarita goes through menopause, and that's too late for the problem that you face now - having a child." The doctor looked at them and said, "I would suggest that you consider adopting children."

Charles's mind raced. Here he was stuck with a "barren cow". He knew his parents would never accept an adopted grandchild. After all the reason he was an only child was because they refused the concept of adoption. They had refused that option when they had been told that they could never have any more children. Could he annul or divorce Margarita, remarry, and have children with someone else? No, that was out of the question. He remembered overhearing a conversation between Margarita and his mother just shortly after their wedding day. His mother had mentioned a situation where if either he or Margarita were ill, like her husband was becoming, would Margarita ever consider a divorce or an annulment. Margarita's answer had come out quickly and forcefully. "Oh, no. Marriage is for life. As a devout Catholic, I'd never ever consider it."

Realizing that he had been sitting there silently, he realized that he had to do something; and, then he knew how he handled this minute was going to be unerasable in both Margarita's and the doctor's minds. He couldn't reveal the pathway which his mind had taken, he couldn't give himself away. His dual-nature kicked in and he said with a huge smile, "Oh my dearest, darling Margarita; it really doesn't matter. Of course, we'll adopt some absolutely wonderful children. You will be the most fantastic mother." He reached over and held his wife tenderly. The doctor smiled and even Margarita managed a small smile.

Wow - he had succeeded in easing the situation. At least that's the way it seemed to all concerned. Inwardly, however, he continued to question what he would really do.

Even on the way home, he continued talking about how they would go about finding the perfect adoptable children. Not one or two, but maybe more. He promised that in between his business trips, he would be searching for associations and organizations who dealt with adoptions. Margarita seemed to accept his words and relaxed. He didn't bother to remind her that his parents had never accepted the idea of adopting children for themselves and, he seriously doubted that they would accept the idea of adopted grandchildren. They had always wanted legitimately birthed heirs for the family and for the business. Why cause more problems for himself, if he could avoid them? He had always been able to think his way out of any situation. He would decide what to do after more thought. Margarita in the meantime seemed content with his reaction and had taken him at his word, as usual.

THE SECRET LIFE OF CHARLES

CHAPTER 5
THE SECRET LIFE OF CHARLES

Life resumed its normal cadence. Other than attempting to find a child or children for adoption, Margarita and Charles went back to their normal routines. Charles found himself traveling even more for business with pleasures wherever he found them on the side. He started to think about what his life could be like without Margarita for a wife. He could neither divorce nor annul the marriage. He could however contemplate her death which would lead to his freedom and chance to marry again - this time with children.

His father's health was failing. Lord Edward continued to turn over more of the business ventures to him which required his constant trips to England. Usually he stayed at his parent's mansion outside London, but occasionally he was forced to stay in town because of late or early business meetings. He therefore bought an apartment in London which basically became his second home away from home.

Several months after again not finding a suitable child for adoption, Charles had to go to England on business. This time because of his mother's insistence, he stayed at his parent's home. He was taken aback by his father's wasted look. Lord Edward had lost at least sixty pounds and his hands shook when he drank from his tea cup. None-the-less his voice was still strong. Now as he spoke to Charles, he was insistent to hear of Margarita and their search for children to adopt. "We must have an heir, if something should happen to you," he stated. "Your mother and I couldn't think of adoption, but perhaps we should have. We put all our eggs in one basket, you," as he pointed directly at Charles. "And now, look, you haven't done your duty to have a son to carry on our line. I'm not getting any younger and neither are you. You have to do something - and quick." Lord Edward's hand dropped to his lap and he seemed to have run out of energy as though the last few moments had sapped what little strength that he possessed.

"There, there," Charles's mother said. "You've worn yourself out again, my dear."

Charles said quietly, "I will, Father; I promise." He left the room and looking back he saw his mother ring for the nurse's aide whom they had hired to help her look after his father.

He went to his room and retrieved from the closet his formal dress attire. There was a dinner at the Prime Minister's that evening which business issues forced him to attend. He wasn't at all sure that he wanted to go, but business was business. Besides, he had to keep up his status in society and, since his father was too ill to go, it fell on him to be present at these affairs of state.

As he was about to descend the staircase, his mother caught him and told him to please give the Prime Minister her regrets about not attending with him. Then silently tearing up, she exclaimed, "I'm so worried about your father. As you can see, he isn't at all well, and I'm afraid your conversation with him has weakened him further. Oh, Charles," and she sobbed, "I don't know how I'll cope without him when he's gone. And I don't think he has much time left. It would give him great joy to have a grandchild."

Charles tenderly kissed his mother's forehead and reminded her that he had promised his father to "do something quickly".

Charles got into his blue Aston Martin and drove into the city. Outside #10 Downey Street he relinquished the car to the attendant and entered to hear soft music and conversation. While the party had started and hors d'oeuvres were being served, the overlarge crowd were drinking wines and mingling before going in to dinner.

As he glanced around the room, his eyes stopped at a group of five people whose center attraction was a striking blonde in an emerald green dress. Her eyes matched her dress. Tall and slender - she was the loveliest woman in the room. Who was she, and how could he meet her? He noticed that she, unlike the other four persons in the group, was not holding a wine glass. Vowing to remedy that problem he moved to the bar and picked up two wineglasses filled with white wine. Why white, he couldn't imagine, but he was an expert in what drinks complimented which people, especially women. She looked like a white wine woman. He carried the glasses over to the group of five; and sipping a small amount from his glass, he offered the other glass to the gorgeous woman. He received a smile and a "thank you" for his efforts. He had been correct. She was definitely a white wine woman.

Little by little he interjected himself into the group's conversation. Slowly the group dispersed one by one to mingle and join other conversations until he stood alone with this ravishing blond. She reminded him of pictures which he had seen of his mother when she had been young - lithe, beautiful, and blond. He was just about to introduce himself when the Prime Minister himself walked over and said, "This is a young woman whom I wanted to introduce you to this evening, but I see you have already met her."

Charles said, "Not yet, but I would love to have an introduction."

The Prime Minister smiled knowingly and said, "Charles, I would like for you to meet my younger sister, Lady Louise Rye, and Lady Louise, this is Lord Charles Elliot whom I told you about yesterday as being someone we need to do business with." Turning to Charles he explained, "Since I became Prime Minister, Louise has been managing all of my family's and my personal business ventures. She is very good at making money."

Charles thought to himself I bet that's not all she's good at. Instead he said aloud, "Lady Louise, I'm so pleased to meet you and will look forward to our cooperative business ventures." If he was any judge of women, and he was, this might be a more memorable evening than he had previously anticipated.

Chapter 5 - The Secret Life of Charles

The bell rang for the guests to enter the dining room for dinner. Charles was delighted that he had been seated next to Louise. She did not eat daintily but tucked in as though she hadn't eaten in weeks. Charles was enjoying the meal and thought that usually a woman's appetite for food was an indication of their sexual appetites. Wow - what a change from Margarita's small appetite and small portions of food.

The meal progressed with everyone at the end of his table discussing everything from military escalations to the recently completed trade agreements with China, India, and the United States. Charles noted that Louise was more than equal to the task, taking issue with some of the more vocal men as they argued the pros and cons of each topic. She was knowledgeable also in domestic matters as the conversation switched to England's economy and evaluation of their British pound against the current European euro, the United States dollar, and the Chinese yen. The comparison of how these currencies were contributing unfavorably to the price of food, gasoline, and durable products like automobiles followed. As he listened to her comments, it seemed that she was highly intelligent and well informed. He could see why the Prime Minister deferred to her business acumen. She was amazing.

Toward the end of the meal as dessert was served, he turned to her and asked quietly, "Are you staying here with your brother?"

She answered, just as quietly, "No, I'm staying at the One Aldwych in Covent Gardens. It's easier than being here. In fact, whenever I'm in London, it becomes my home."

"Where is your real home?" Charles asked.

"In the Cotswold's, where it's more serene, has an ocean view, and is away from the hubbub of downtown London and its suburbs."

"Do you live there with your husband?"

"Oh, no, with my child. My husband was killed in an automobile accident several years ago."

"So, you're single?"

"Yes, and you? Are you married?"

Charles hesitated for a minute before answering, "Yes, unfortunately. Does it make a difference?"

Glancing quickly around the table to see if anyone was listening to their quiet conversation and seeing that no one was paying attention to them, Louise answered, "No, not in the least. You are the most handsome man here, and I'd love to get to know you better - in business and personally."

"The feeling is mutual", he replied. "Might I be permitted to take you to your hotel when this evening is over?"

"I was hoping that you would ask," she replied.

As the men retired to the drawing room for cigars and brandy and the women started moving toward the salon for sweets, Charles whispered to her, "When this is over, I'll leave first and get the car, so that when you come out, I'll drive up and pick you up."

She whispered back, "I'll be looking for you."

The rest of the evening flew by. At last the departure occurred. True to his word, Charles left quickly and retrieved his car, pulling into the line with limos which were picking up the departing quests. Louise came out, glanced down the lines of cars, saw him, and quickly came to the car. She opened the door and climbed in, even before he could be the gentleman and open the door for her. He wondered if she were as anxious to be with him as he was to be with her.

As she got in, she said, "I thought the evening would never be over."

"Me too," he answered.

The drive to the hotel took little time and as he pulled up to the entrance, he asked, "May I accompany you inside?"

"No," she answered, getting out quickly. "Just go park the car and come in; I'm in Suite 22".

Charles followed her instructions and arrived about ten

minutes later. He didn't have to knock. She must have been at the keyhole waiting for him as she quickly opened the door.

He entered and they embraced passionately with a kiss.

"I've wanted you to kiss me all night," she said.

"And, I've wanted to kiss YOU all night," he replied.

They kissed again. This time as if it were the most obvious sequence of events for them.

She led him over to the table in the center of the room where there was an ice bucket already filled with ice and a bottle of champagne. Next to it were two crystal champagne flutes. She indicated that he should sit on a nearby couch and as he did so, there was a knock at the door which she went to answer. When she opened the door, a bellboy came in wheeling a small serving table with a second ice bucket and bottle of champagne, a bowl of assorted fruits, and a tray of small sandwiches. Charles thought she had either ordered these things on the way up to her room or as soon as she had gotten there.

As the boy left, she said, "I thought we might be thirsty; and we might also work up an appetite."

He laughed and said, "You might be right." He reached over, took the bottle of champagne from its ice bucket on the table, and poured the two flutes with champagne. As he handed her one and took one himself, he toasted them, saying, "To our future joint enterprises."

"I'm looking forward to all of them," she answered, giving him a sly sideways glance.

They slowly sipped from their glasses while gazing at each other. She reached for one of the small sandwiches, and then, so did he. They were delicious. It had been quite a while since dinner and they had both eaten a lot, but it seemed that they were both able to eat again. The first flutes were empty by then, so he refilled them.

"Do you mind if I slip into something a bit more casual?" She asked.

"Be my guest."

As she left the room, he took off his jacket and bowtie and unbuttoned the top two buttons of his shirt. He thought that if she was to be more relaxed, so would he. He wasn't sure about where she was leading, but he was more than willing to play along. This might indeed be a very profitable evening. He had nowhere he had to be, and she was so beautiful. He took another sip of champagne. He heard the bedroom door open and looked up. If he had thought she was beautiful in the emerald green ballgown, she was even more beautiful as she entered the sitting room. She was barefoot and was wearing a pale apricot-colored negligee and nightgown. It almost looked as though she was nude - but not quite. Her blond hair fell in waves to her shoulders. She was enticing. He thought she might be even more enticing totally nude. Maybe he could rectify that.

She came over, picked up her glass, and took another sip as she sat down in a chair directly opposite, but very near and at an angle from him. As she tucked her feet under her, she said softly, "Now, where were we?"

"Talking of joint enterprises and mergers, "he said, smiling at her.

"Oh, yes. I remember now. And, where and when were all of these to take place?" she asked coyly as she moved to sit on the couch with him.

"Perhaps there, or better still, here," he responded.

"And perhaps after a little more champagne?"

"Louise, my dear, we have all night to decide; and, after all, this is your suite, so you call the shots."

"No - please no shots," she said laughingly. "We're drinking champagne, not whiskey."

Then they were both laughing. The serious beginning mood of their visit was over. Now it became two very close friends, who were to be even closer, laughing at a private joke and enjoying each other's company. They ate a couple more sandwiches and sipped more champagne. She was easy to talk to, but the champagne seemed to be going to both their heads, as she moved to sit right next to him.

At last she stood up, and, taking his hand in hers, she led the way to the bedroom where they undressed each other slowly. At last they entered the bed itself. It seemed the most natural thing to both of them. Their desire increased as they explored each other's body; and, finally, their bodies joined in an explosion of passion.

With bodies wet with the sweat of love-making, they now relaxed and clung to each other. She laid her head on his chest. His arms held her tenderly as he stroked her back. She kissed his chest. He kissed her forehead gently, then her neck, and then both breasts. Never before had Charles met his match in love-making; but Louise was indeed a woman to be admired in many ways. He had thought he admired her mind, but tonight he had found that he admired her body equally.

Their love making continued for the remaining hours of the night and lasted into the early hours of the morning. Exhausted, they fell asleep in a tangled mass of arms and legs, each fully satiated by the other.

Late morning light sifted into the room through a crack in the curtains. She languidly rolled over on her back and said, "I'm hungry; how about you?"

In wonderment, he looked over at her. She was more lovely nude than clothed. How had he gotten so lucky?

With never a thought of Margarita, he answered, "I think I'd like a shower first."

She said, "Only if it's a two-person shower."

"Then save room for me," he responded.

An hour later and another love making session having been completed in the shower, he said, "Now I'm hungry."

She went into the living room and called down an order for breakfast for two composed of sausage, bacon, eggs, potatoes, juice, and coffee, while he dressed. Within a short time, a sumptuous breakfast arrived from room service. He was thoroughly impressed with the way she had ordered without even asking him what he had wanted. He thought here is a woman who is clearly exacting, confident, resourceful, and used to knowing what she wants and knowing how to get it. What a delightful surprise.

When they had finished the breakfast, he said, "I really need to get to the office and get to work. Unfortunately, I need to go home and change clothes."

"Me too", she replied.

"When can we be together again?" he asked.

"I have to return to my cottage today, but I'll be back in London in two weeks. Then we can discuss mergers," she said laughing, "both in business and like this. Call me two weeks from today. Ask for my suite and I'll be here".

As he drove to his parents' mansion, he mused. Here was a woman who not only intrigued him but was everything he could desire. And - she, having a son, had proven herself to be fertile. Maybe his friends, who had been to Africa, were right when they cited the cultural tradition in African tribes whose men wouldn't marry a woman until she had already had a child to signify her fertility. Too bad that he had married Margarita without such a guarantee.

As he entered his parents' house, he met his mother in the hallway. She looked at her watch and commented "Late night."

He answered, "Yes. I spent the night in my London apartment instead of coming here." Thinking to himself he said that yes, the next time, he WOULD spend the night in his own apartment - but with Louise.

She remarked, "But you didn't change clothes there."

He dismissed her remark with a slight wave of his hand. Then he went up to his room quickly to dress for a business day.

She went into the library where her housekeeper found

her. "Lady Anne, you have a call from Lady Mary Roberts, ma'am."

Lady Anne went to the phone and said, "Hello Mary, how are you?"

"I'm really very well, thank you. I was so sorry that you and Lord Edward were unable to attend the dinner at the Prime Minister's last night; but I supposed Edward wasn't up to it."

"No, he's not doing well these days."

"I was gratified to see Charles there. You must be very proud of him and his ability to stand in for his father."

"Oh yes, he is quite able."

"And his wife - I understand that she hasn't been well of late and usually stays in their home near Madrid."

"Yes, they're in the process of adopting some children. She's had a dreadful time conceiving. Charles has been very attentive to her and is so concerned. He realizes that his social status requires an heir."

"Oh, I'm terribly sorry to hear that; however, he didn't seem preoccupied last night."

"He puts on a brave front", his mother replied.

"Yes. He seemed to be speaking to many people last night, especially to the Prime Minister's younger sister, who is quite business minded."

"I had forgotten that the Prime Minister had more than one sister."

"Yes, they seemed really engrossed in conversation."

"Mary, I fear that I must cut this conversation short, Lord Edward just called to me, and I need to tend to him. Please forgive the brevity of our conversation".

"Oh, my dear, I understand completely what with Lord Edward's condition. Anne, do you have plans for next week?"

"Yes, we are going to the south coast to enable Edward to have some sun and fresh sea air. I'm hoping that he will be much improved when we return in two weeks. I realize that it is such a limited vacation time, but when I made arrangements, the seaside hotel was practically booked solid. I could only arrange two weeks. We'll have to plan a longer trip later if Edward does well this time and wants to return."

"I certainly hope so. Call me when you return and we'll have tea."

As the phone call ended Charles's mother thought about Charles and the news that she had just received. Evidently, he wasn't living the faithful husband role that he was pretending to. It sounded like he had resumed his "playboy" bachelor conquests from his younger years. She vowed to be a little more diligent in keeping tabs on him. He was surely up to no good if he was romancing the Prime Minister's younger sister.

CHAPTER 6

MARGARITA S LIFE

CHAPTER 6

MARGARITA'S LIFE

The days dragged along - every one the same, especially when Charles was gone on his many business trips. Margarita found herself dwelling more and more on her inadequacy as a woman. As a result, she turned to the one thing in her life that had always brought solace, her faith in God.

She started attending mass daily. The smell of incense and burning candles, the ritual of the mass, and the bowed heads of others gave her the sense of belonging to something bigger than her daily life. When she made her weekly confession, Padre Juan comforted her with his quiet, gentle words. She felt a peace that she hadn't known since childhood. She started to help at the church's school with the younger children and prayed that someday she too would have a child that could attend.

When she had gotten the news that she indeed was barren, she had prayed even harder that they would be able to find a child to adopt to fulfill this need. But Charles was so busy with work that she sometimes felt that he wasn't trying very hard to find the right adoption organization to help them. Voicing this thought during her confession, she decided that she was being unfair to her husband and it made her feel all the more guilty. First, she was guilty that she couldn't conceive and now she was guilty that she blamed Charles for not finding a place to adopt. How had their life come to this? They had been so happy when they were married. Now it seemed like they were looking for ways to find fault with each other and to find times to be apart. She wondered if they were ever going to be happy again. When she was in church, she was upset; and, when she was home, she also was equally upset. She pondered how often she had recently found herself weeping alone in the garden.

Chapter 6 - Margarita's Life

Several times during the last few months she had gone to Mallorca to be with her parents, but they were older now and she tried not to worry them. Her older brother had basically taken over the auto repair business and had no time for her. Her other brothers and sisters were all so busy with their own lives and families that they had little time for her either. Plus, when she looked at all of their little ones, it only made it harder on her that she couldn't have a little one of her own. She, who had been the favored child, with everything now going on in her life, found herself the unfavored of God. She was on the outside looking in. She decided that she'd make no more trips "home" in the future. These trips to Mallorca only seemed to make her more unhappy and self-deprecating. What was she to do?

She really had no friends in the village or in the Toledo or Madrid area so she decided she'd start going to the library, get some books, and read. She had so loved to read when she was younger. She soon became a friend of the librarian who recommended books to her. One day while she went to find a book, she walked by the newspapers and news magazines area. Her eyes landed on the cover picture of El Mundo. She couldn't believe it. The photo was taken at a dinner party at the English Prime Minister's home in London. In the background was Charles with a beautiful blond woman in a green dress. While the caption was one of the guests discussing business and while Charles and the woman were not named nor the focal point of the photo, Margarita saw her husband's facial expression. It was one she knew so well. It was the enraptured face which she had seen him bestow upon her when he had been courting her. Could he be involved with this woman? What was he up to? Something was amiss.

Never before had she ever questioned his fidelity. Never before had she ever wondered about his many business trips that took him away from her. When she went home, she took her calendar and a pad of paper and started listing all the dates of his many business trips during the last five years (even before they were married). She had always known to keep a calendar to time his trips, when he would be home or not, and when her ovulations would occur so that when he was at home, perhaps they could try to conceive a child. Somehow, she had never really looked at the number of days that he had left her alone and traveled abroad. She had been more interested in the number of days that he was at home. On the list she added the locations that he had told her that his business dealings were being held. While she had kept track of them, so that she would always look her best, orchestrate the best meals, and anticipate his homecomings, what had he been planning and doing?

The next day, armed with her list, she went to the librarian and asked about back issues of El Mundo and other newspapers and periodicals. The librarian directed her to a reading room to the left of the main library desk and showed her how she could find what she wanted by date.

Sure enough! Many of the dates of his business trips found those same dates memorialized with his photo with various women in the gossip or society columns at those same places all over the globe. Charles had been a very busy and, she mused, naughty boy. He was not the wonderful, faithful husband that he had led her to believe. She had believed him and in him. Now she knew better. But what was she to do?

She went to mass and then confession. In confession Padre Juan gave her advice that priests had always given to women in the same straits. "You need to pray harder, child."

For the first time in her life she questioned her religion. How in all sincerity could a priest, who isn't allowed to marry, give a reliable piece of advice on marriage, especially a marriage which was "going south". Maybe the Jewish and Christian religions were more realistic, allowing their rabbis and ministers the right to marry. At least they would be more likely to know about married couples and their problems.

Charles wasn't due to be home for several days yet. Could she find a rabbi or a minister to talk to about this problem?

Chapter 6 - Margarita's Life

Looking in the phone directory, she saw that the nearest synagogue was across in Madrid, but the nearest protestant church was only eight blocks away. She could walk that distance easily. Going into Madrid would be too noticeable.

The next morning, she told the housekeeper that she felt that she needed some exercise and was going for a walk. She found the address she was looking for and was disappointed. It wasn't a fine structure like her Catholic church. In fact, it looked rather shabby. Regardless, she went to the front door, but it was locked. She read the sign which directed her to a side entrance with a bell, which she rang. A gentle looking man opened the door to her and inquired as to what she wanted. She answered, "To speak to your priest or minister - whatever he is called."

"I'm the minister here," he answered. "My name is Pastor Luis. Do you need to speak now or do you wish to make an appointment?"

"May we speak now?"

"Of course, my child."

The next hour Margarita poured out her heart to this strange preacher. She even showed him some of the evidence which she had accumulated. She learned that indeed he was married, was kindhearted, and was very easy to talk to.

His words were, "Perhaps you're reading more into your findings than have merit. My advice is to go home, carefully watch your husband and his actions. Don't confront him, as he will deny any wrongdoing. It is better to be cautious than confrontational. As time goes by and you accumulate more evidence of his unfaithfulness, then it is time to talk with him about your findings. You have only recently begun to suspect him with what appears to be circumstantial evidence. Don't be so quick to jump to conclusions without hard evidence. Wait and see what happens next. You've been patient with his business trips all this time. He doesn't know you're suspicious. Give him some time. If he is guilty of what you suspect, he will ultimately be revealed and show his true actions and motives. If you find we need to talk again, please come see me."

Margarita recognized the good advice that she was receiving. Yes, perhaps she had jumped to conclusions. And maybe those conclusions were wrong. She'd wait. She also realized that usually her instincts were correct. She'd continue to track down his time away from her. But she also realized that this minister had understood her and her problems better than her priest had.

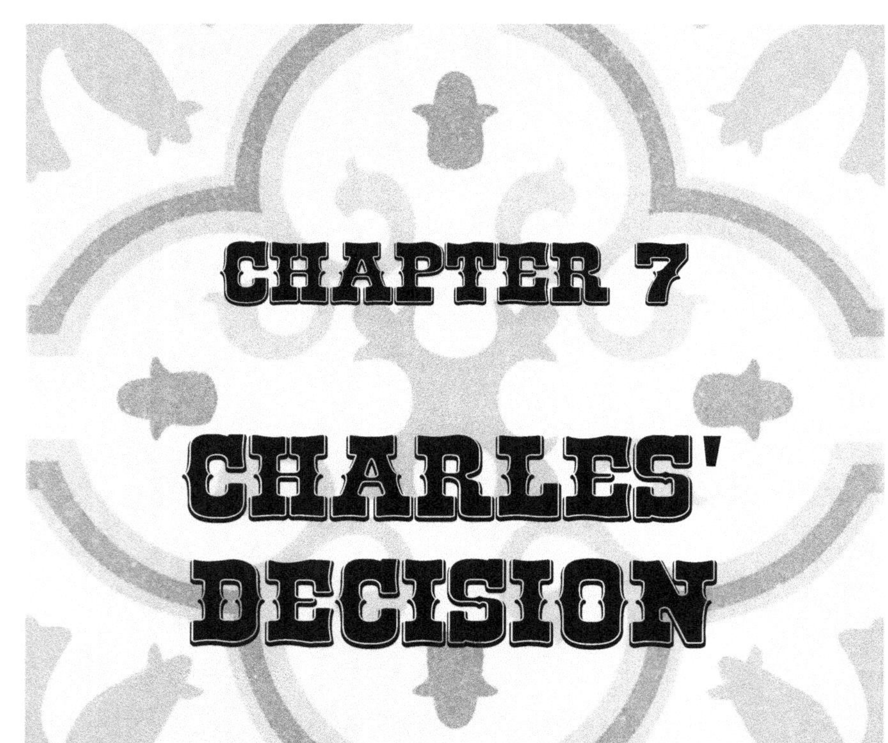

CHAPTER 7

CHARLES' DECISION

CHAPTER 7

CHARLES' DECISION

Two days later Charles came home all smiles and bearing her two gifts, a beautiful gold necklace and matching earrings with garnets set in exquisitely roped settings. They looked lovely on her. He then told her of an orphanage in England who were anxious to start an adoption process for them. After he had left Louise two days earlier, he had started to call around the London area to research names of adoptions places. Although he had been telling Margarita that he had been looking all over for appropriate adoption agencies, he really hadn't done any such thing, as in his mind, he couldn't imagine adopting a child. While he hadn't called this English agency when he found their name, nor even really knew if they could adopt there, the fact that he had brought home a name of some place where they could potentially adopt would make it look to Margarita that he had been thinking of her while he had been away. He had always known how to keep her happy.

Charles had made several decisions while he had been away and after he had met the wonderfully captivating Lady Louise. The first decision was to follow through on his past history of showing two faces to the world, but now it meant continuing to show two faces to his wife. He had been good at that when he had first courted her, with her spending the year as Miss World, while he carried on as if he were a bachelor. He would make her believe that he could obtain a child, or children, for them and that he loved her as deeply as he had when he had first pursued her.

His second decision was to kill her.

Since he couldn't divorce her or annul the marriage, there was a way to get rid of her. He always got what he wanted, and he wanted Lady Louise. He no longer wanted his wife. She had become a huge disappointment to him. Even though she was still beautiful and loved him, she couldn't bear a child. His parents and society dictated that the family have an heir. He had promised his father that he would do something and do it quickly. It was almost like a deathbed request and promise which he had made, considering the physical and mental condition of his invalid father.

As to how to carry out this second decision became the focus of his next planning. He knew that he couldn't count on someone else to do the job. People talked. Sooner or later he would be found out as having planned the murder, whether he personally did it or not. Might as well be hanged as a horse instead of a mule - it was the same. He remembered his father's words, "If you want something done right, do it yourself." Of course, his father had meant doing something in business, but those words also applied to everything else. He then consulted with his old Mafia friends in Italy. He had always been able to obtain anything from anywhere when he used their connections. Having used their services before, he knew they were reliable - for a price. With this problem, price was no object. He told them that he wanted at least two passports, - no, four would be better. All the passports needed different names and photos of him in different disguises. He would also need associated credit cards and business cards so that wherever and whenever he would be stopped, he could back up the different identities. These passports were now in the process of being made, but he would have to make a trip to Italy to have the photos taken. He had described the kinds of disguises that he would require and they were also getting those for him. He hadn't lost his touch. Once he made up his mind, he could accomplish lots of things which other people later saw as miracles. A week later his friends called him from Italy saying that he could come and get his merchandise.

He had also decided that as soon as Margarita was eliminated, he would marry Lady Louise. In the meantime, every time he went to London, on business of course, he would spend some very productive hours with her in his London apartment or at her hotel. He would court her, just as ardently as he had courted Margarita. The result would be that he would have a beautiful and fertile wife; he could merge her business sense to his; he would have an "in" with the Prime Minister himself, who ultimately would be wrapped around his little finger as a relative; and he could count on becoming a Lord in the House of Lords on his own merit and not rely on his father's name and title. Life would be very good indeed.

He had thought long and hard. He needed a plan that would include a "fall person" who could be prosecuted for his crime. He had to plan carefully enough to provide a way to get into his home in Spain "without being there" and out and place himself with a foolproof alibi about where he had actually been during the murder. Again, he would attempt the impossible and would succeed. He knew that he was smart enough to do it. It was a matter of being two people at once; something he had done his entire life.

The last time he had been in Amsterdam he had gone into several art museums and had fallen in love with paintings of Van Eyck. He had especially liked the painting "The Arnolfini Marriage". The docent had told his tourist group about the symbolism in the painting. Each object was subtly hidden but held very significant meanings. A subterfuge. He liked that. It was like him - out in the open, but also hidden. That would be the way his murder of Margarita would be - transparent, but opaque. He started to develop his foolproof plan, because he would never be found out.

He decided that he would flatter Margarita by having an artist paint her portrait. While she knew that he and most other people thought of her as an especially beautiful woman, she herself didn't always seem to be conceited enough to think of herself as beautiful. Even with all the pageants that she had won. She would think that he was totally enthralled with, captivated by, and committed to her; and, that he wanted to express his love and devotion by celebrating her upcoming birthday. She would be tied up time-wise with sittings, thinking nothing of what he was doing otherwise than planning for a huge celebration. He had already led her to believe that his extra time from business was spent in finding a child to adopt.

Now, he had to find an artist whom he could commission to actually paint a portrait. It must be someone unknown; someone who would jump at the chance to paint somebody important; someone who needed money badly; someone who wouldn't question his motives or how he wanted the portrait done; someone who wouldn't wonder at the setting; and someone whom he could "sweet talk" into taking on a long-term project with the hope of future reward.

In the meantime, he started to plan how he would cover his tracks - leaving his parents' home, going to Spain, committing the murder, and getting back to England. By leaving from his parent's home, he would establish an airtight alibi. Not only his parents, but their live-in staff would be able to verify his whereabouts during the murder. He would have to be sure that his "stand in" murderer would not have an alibi. Maybe he could even point a finger at them in some way that there would be no doubt about them being the guilty person - capable of the crime. It would be ideal if his "murderer" were also the artist. That would kill two birds with one stone.

He couldn't be obtuse in his search for such an artist. He, no matter where he was, would be on the lookout for one. Unfortunately, he couldn't inquire from friends or acquaintances for such a person because he didn't want to leave any loose ends where people could start following his plans.

One morning he began to complain to Margarita that he had been too busy working to exercise frequently. In order to lose a few pounds, he decided to begin walking back and forth to the village. In reality he needed to know exactly how he could come and go unseen, where he could hide transportation, how much time he needed to get from one location to another, and precisely how he could quickly kill and vanish. The village was built on a hill above the train station and the river. His villa sat near the top of the hill and was only accessible via ancient streets that were little more than one-lane alleyways. A car was out of the question due to difficulty of use and lack of stealth. Parking was at a minimum and most of the villagers knew their neighbors' cars and would recognize a strange vehicle. He had to have a bicycle.

On his next trip into Madrid, he found what he was looking for - an old bicycle with scraped red paint, rusty, and bent, but it looked to be in good working order. It was in a thrift shop and he saw it only through the store window. He thought for a moment; then, realizing that the bicycle might later be found with questions asked about its purchase, he didn't go into the shop. It was too bad that he didn't have any of the disguises that he had ordered from his friends in Italy. He didn't want to be identified by the store's owner. He reviewed the different descriptions which he had sent to Italy for the various disguises. Picking the easiest one to duplicate, he went into a store for children's party costumes and came out having purchased a black wig, horned-rimmed glasses. fake mustache, and scissors. In a public restroom he trimmed the wig so that it was longer than his own hair, but still a respectable length. He then returned to the thrift store and purchased the bicycle. He paid cash so that a credit card and identification weren't necessary. He had parked his car about a mile from the store, and looking around and seeing no one, he quickly put the bike into the car's boot. On the way home he put the scissors, glasses, and black wig in his briefcase. Upon reaching home, he stored the bicycle in the garage under some old tarpaulins. He felt secure that his escape vehicle was ready now.

He studied the train schedules between London and Paris, Paris and Madrid, and Madrid and Toledo. Even though there were more direct routes which he could take, they were slow. The trains which he was considering were all rapid transit ones. The distances were greater, but the transit times were shorter in duration. He had to adhere to his timetable. He figured especially going under the English Channel on the train was much better than trying to take ferries over the channel to and from Bilbao. He couldn't risk airplanes with all their checking of passports, wait times, and regulations. With planes, one still had to find ground transportation once one arrived and that presented another set of problems. No, he was better sticking to going by train. He concluded with his schedule and discovered that he could leave London early evening and get to Toledo on the last train. It would be pitch black at night and he could walk to the village and up the hill to the alley behind the villa without being seen. By the time he had murdered Margarita, biked back to the village, ditched the bike in the river, continued walking to the train station in Toledo, and taken the very first train out of Toledo, he could be home in England sometime between nine and noon the next day. If he could think of some plausible reason, he might even be able to leave England earlier and give himself even more time. He was glad that he had ordered four different disguises because that would enable him to change disguises with each different train. No one would ever be able to trace him. With twenty-four hours, little sleep, and swift action, he would be free of Margarita and be able to marry Louise. Even if Louise never conceived again, he would adopt her child, and have an heir to please his parents.

The next step was to find a proper artist and finish his plans.

CHAPTER 8

PORTRAIT DETAILS

CHAPTER 8
PORTRAIT DETAILS

After Charles Elliot had walked off from the café, I, Marielena Cortez Diez, sat stunned for the next hour. I wondered what I had gotten myself into. Finally, I decided that the best of the bargain that I had just struck was that I'd have steady money coming in for a change. This was going to be the biggest challenge of my artistic life. Maybe this was the break which I'd been waiting for. I had only been able to paint part-time in Rhonda, because I was forced to pay bills with income from a low-paying job in a small clothing store. This decision to devote myself fulltime to art had been momentous. Many of my fellow artists from my art education classes had made the same decision but had later regretted it. Perhaps they, as my mother had warned, weren't able to make a living on only their art. Only time would tell if I could succeed. Nothing else on the horizon was as promising as this new commission.

Charles Elliot had instructed me at the conclusion of our lengthy meeting at the cafe to report to his home on Tuesday so that I could meet his wife. I had agreed. I remembered how he had been very clear in describing how he wanted the commission painted, in fact the entire conversation was as though it had taken place in a movie so that I could remember every word. I had thought about how difficult it would actually be to accomplish. First, it was to be a full-frontal portrait of his wife standing beside a table near an open balcony door and a table.

"You are, of course, familiar with Jan van Eyck's painting entitled 'Giovanni Arnolfini and His Wife' or the 'Arnolfini Wedding'?" he had asked me.

"Of course. It is very well known," was my reply.

"Well, I have grown to love it. I want to have some of

the same types of symbolism in Margarita's portrait as in that painting. With only one person, my wife, in it and not a couple." He continued, "Van Eyck used light as an important tool as well as his structuring of background details."

I nodded my head in agreement, realizing that Charles was a knowledgeable art connoisseur to understand these technicalities of composition.

"This portrait is to be a formal one just like the Van Eyck painting and will be placed in the very large foyer of my villa so that anyone entering the villa will be struck by my wife's beauty and my love for her. She was Miss Spain and Miss World, you know."

I again nodded, although I previously had no idea who his wife was; but all Spain would know. I was suddenly startled by the realization of what I was attempting to accomplish with this portrait.

He continued, "The measurements of the canvas will be three meters tall by two meters wide - quite large. I understand you work in oils?"

"No," I replied, "in acrylics. Does that matter?"

"No, in fact that would be better, since I know that they dry very fast and, research has recently stated, that acrylic paintings will last much longer than oil paintings. Furthermore, Margarita's birthday is only six weeks away and I want the painting finished quickly.":

"You mentioned a celebration?" I asked questioningly.

"Yes, and the painting absolutely has to be finished prior to that celebration."

"And how will she be dressed in the portrait?"

"I have purchased a garnet-colored, full-length, silk evening dress. The balcony door will be open in the painting which will show the flower gardens outside. The flowers there will also show the same color, plus other complementary colors, that are in her dress."

"And the rest of the painting?" I asked.

"The table next to the balcony doors will hold the symbolic items depicting a loving, successful married life. But you will see those items when you come on Tuesday since I have already decided on those items, some of which I still have to purchase. I'm hoping that you can do some preliminary sketches when you come."

I agreed to bring my sketchbook and a camera to take close-ups of a variety of things, including his wife, the table, the gardens, the balcony, and its door.

As I sat there, I started to make a list of all the materials in my sketchbook that I would need to purchase with the down payment monies. While the list was not all that extensive, the one item that I might have to make myself was the two by three metered canvas. Then I was startled with the realization that I had no means of even transporting such a huge canvas - nor an easel of that size to paint it on. My first step would have to be to obtain both of these in Madrid, custom- made, and have them shipped to the villa. I couldn't possibly build such a canvas and easel, nor transport them. I also wouldn't have the luxury of working on the portrait in my own studio/apartment. It was much too small, and the stairway leading up to it, wouldn't accommodate the huge canvas. All these ideas began to give me the premonition of the enormity of the task at hand - and in only six weeks? I hoped that I would be able to get along with his wife as we'd be spending a lot of time together in the next five and a half weeks.

Questions emerged: Would I like his wife? Would she like me? Would she respect my silences as I contemplated my next brushstroke? Would she not interrupt my thought process as I tried to capture her likeness, both in feature and in personality?' Would she respect my times alone working with the canvas, paints, and brushes? And where was Charles going to be during my time spent at the villa? Would his interruptions hinder me?

I put in a call to the best art supplies store in Madrid with a full description of what I would have to have. After the call, I drew in a huge sigh; the cost of the canvas and the easel were exceedingly more than I had anticipated. The delivery charges were so outrageous that I soon realized that I'd have to be frugal to make ends meet. What had appeared to be a huge windfall of income had shrunk to practically nothing. I had no choice. I definitely had to finish the commission and do it quickly. Otherwise, I would have no income at all. I had thought that I'd made a shrewd deal. Not really! Not only that, but I needed to pay my rent during the entire time and to eat during the entire time that I would be working on the portrait. I set aside the rent money from the amount that I would need for the supplies and took it down to my landlady, Señora Santiago so that at least the rent would be paid in advance.

Not being a commission-oriented artist, I had not considered the total costs involved. Furthermore, if Charles didn't like the portrait, when it was finished, he could refuse to pay the remaining amount. No wonder he had been so anxious to seal the deal. I hated to think what would happen to me, both financially and reputationally as an artist, if I failed to meet his expectations. At least, I had made it a point that this fifty percent, the down payment, was non-refundable. I would have really been stupid not to do so. If he didn't like the portrait when it was finished, I still wouldn't be driving myself into deeper debt; but, I worried, I would not have any money left to live on.

I nervously called the art supply store again and emphasized that the easel and canvas had to be delivered to the villa the first thing on Tuesday morning. Of course, I would have to un-crate them and set up the easel myself, but I knew how to do that.

CHAPTER 9

INTRODUCTIONS

CHAPTER 9

INTRODUCTIONS

Marielena reported to the villa early Tuesday morning and discovered that the delivery men from the art supply store were already unloading the crates containing the canvas and easel from the delivery van. Charles met her at the door and directed the men to take the crates and follow them to the second-floor room which would become her studio for the next five and a half weeks. She followed along not knowing what exactly to expect. Would the room be large, have adequate lighting, and be an asset in the portrait?

The villa was huge, as had been the surrounding grounds. When she had entered the walled and gated entry from the narrow road on her way from the village, she had been impressed with the expanse of the villa. And the view, even from the road, had been breathtaking as she had climbed up the hill. The light-colored stucco walls gave the entire villa a warm golden, romantic look which continued from the outside into the interior foyer. A large, blank wall confronted her when she entered through the heavy oak and metal bracketed door. She assumed this large wall was where her canvas would be placed. There would be absolutely no way that anyone entering the villa could miss Charles's wife's portrait. To the right of the foyer was an enormous salon whose walls were lined with many paintings. Although she couldn't see them in detail, they all looked to be original artworks with beautiful gold-leafed frames. She turned to Charles and asked, "I see that all your paintings here have gold-leaf frames; have you envisioned how you will be framing your wife's portrait?"

He answered, "In gold, of course, but I will see to that after the portrait is finished. I know that a frame can make or break a piece of art, so first the painting and then the frame. We'll have plenty of time to decide that later."

The foyer had an elegant curving staircase on the left where they climbed up to the second floor. Perhaps his wife's birthday celebration would take place in the right hand salon and foyer. High niches in the walls allowed air to circulate and light to enter at interesting angles. The morning was going to be very hot, but the villa's thick walls and air currents would keep the rooms cool, even on the hottest of days. That would be much better working conditions than she had in her attic studio in the village. The coolness would make painting the commission easier to endure. Everywhere there were tiled floors which would be cooler too. She could imagine that she might possibly even enjoy painting in her bare feet against the cool tiles.

As they continued to climb the staircase, it arched back toward the right, ending in a second-floor crosswalk overhanging the foyer's blank wall. This crosswalk would conceal the portrait below from the second floor. They entered a long hallway, which stretched back toward the back of the villa from the crosswalk. She estimated that this hallway was located approximately in the center of the villa. At the hallway's far end on the right were two doors separated by approximately 10 meters. Charles, Marielena, and the two delivery men entered the first of the doors and went into an enormous room. The delivery men asked where to set the crates and Charles indicated near the door which they had just entered. Setting the crates down, the men excused themselves and left the room the same way in which they had entered.

Marielena looked with curiosity at the room. To her left and toward the back of the room was a second door. She assumed that this was the second door which she had seen in the hallway; therefore, this room had two entrances, the one they had entered and another further toward the back of the room. The far wall contained a window on the left, near this second door, and floor to ceiling drapes, which covered the remaining wall space. They walked together to these draperies. As Charles pulled the heavy brocade curtains open to the right, a huge entryway with double-doors became exposed. Beyond these double doors, which he also proceeded to open, was a balcony overlooking the gardens. From the balcony were another set of circular stairs descending into the gardens below.

As she stood looking at the entire view, both interior and exterior, Charles explained "I know this isn't the norm for Spanish villas. It looks more Italian. During the year when Margarita was Miss World, we saw villas like this one on the Amalfi coast. We both loved how these villas were constructed; so, when I purchased this villa, I had it transformed into a more Italian-like one with the balcony, balcony doors, and outside staircase."

He was correct, she thought. Perhaps it was the reason why he had chosen this room for the portrait's background. She mused, What a beautiful setting!

As she slowly walked around the room, she immediately saw a couple of problems. She remembered that Charles had stated that his wife would be standing near the table on the left with the doors leading to the balcony on her right. In that position his wife would be back-lit by a combination of light coming from the window and the doors behind her. To remedy that problem, there would have to be additional lights in front, so as to front-light his wife. The second problem was that she would need additional lights behind her so as to be able to see the canvas to paint. As she pointed out these problems, Charles stated, "Those will be no problems at all, I will have additional lights installed immediately."

As he was speaking, the door closest to the table opened and in walked one of the most beautiful women that Marielena had ever seen.

"Ah," said Charles, "here is your subject, Marielena. Let me introduce my wife. Margarita Ruiz Mendoza Serrano Nadal meet your artist, Marielena Cortez Diez Sanchez Francisco. Marielena, this is my wife Margarita."

As the two women kissed each other on both cheeks in greeting, Charles continued, "You'll be spending a lot of time together in the future. I hope you will also become friends." He pointed toward the table and the windows and said to his wife, "You will be standing here close to the table, but between the table and the doors for the portrait. Your right hand will be resting lightly on the table and your left hand will be on your stomach, like the Van Eyck painting which I like so much. Your back will be to the door and you will be facing into the room."

She smiled at Marielena sweetly and said, "He always seems to know exactly what he wants."

Marielena answered, "Let me get my camera and sketchbook from my bag, and I will start my sketches immediately."

Charles said, "I'll leave you ladies to get started while I obtain the necessary lights."

As Marielena retrieved the camera and sketchbook, Margarita stared out at the garden. She quickly wiped a tear from her eye.

"Is there anything wrong?" Marielena asked.

"No, I only have a touch of hay fever and allergies," Margarita responded. "Now where do you want me to stand - anywhere or beside the table?"

"Let's start with the pose that your husband wants with you near the table," said Marielena. Marielena started to move about the room taking photos of the door, the entire room, and Margarita near the table. Then she took her sketchbook and did a very quick sketch of Margarita in the place that she would be in the portrait. "I'm going to do a much more detailed sketch now and it will take some time. If you get tired, we can sit on the couch over there and rest."

After a half hour, they rested for a while, and then began again. Marielena finished the detailed sketch and then explained, "After this next break, I will do some more quick sketches in different positions and take some more photos." An hour later, the second door opened again and the housekeeper came in with a pitcher of cold lemonade and a tray of sandwiches.

"I thought we might need these about this time so I had Paula bring them up from the kitchen," said Margarita, indicating the housekeeper. "Marielena, this is my housekeeper, Paula. She will be around if you need anything while you're here."

"Mucho gusto", Marielena said to the housekeeper. And turning to Margarita, she added, "Oh, how thoughtful; I was getting thirsty". They laughed together as if they had read each other's minds.

Sitting together on the sofa, Margarita asked, "Tell me about yourself?"

"There isn't much to tell," replied Marielena. "I've been doing artwork my entire life. I was a sickly child and spent a lot of my days growing up with books, crayons, pencils, and paper. I enjoyed doing that so much that when I grew up, I decided to become an artist. As you might guess, it isn't the most forgiving vocation. One laughs at the phrase 'starving artist' but there really is some truth to the phrase."

"But do you enjoy it?" asked Margarita.

"Oh, yes, but there are times when I don't eat well and when I'm working just to pay the rent. The last village that I lived in wasn't affluent so I also had a job for a while in a bar as a waitress and later another job in a small clothing store just before I moved here. When I moved here, I was hoping that I could devote myself entirely to my art. I was sketching in a café when your husband saw my work and commissioned me to paint your portrait."

"Where do you live?"

"I have a small attic room in the old town at the home of Señora Santiago. I'm squeezed into it with a bed, table, chair, and my easel. It's the best I can do right now." Marielena added quickly, "Oh, don't get me wrong. I'll be doing better as I am here longer and develop a clientele. I'm really not as destitute as that sounded."

Chapter 9 - Introductions

Margarita sighed and said, "No, I do understand. My family in Mallorca was not wealthy either. There were six of us children. My father was a mechanic, and my mother a cashier in a store, 'en una tienda'. She had several miscarriages as well as us six children to care for. We had to live with very little. This," she indicated the room in which they sat, "would have been two times as big in size as the size of our whole house." She sighed again, "I've only lived in this luxury since I married Charles."

As they finished the sandwiches Marielena said, "I need to do some sketches of just your face, your hands, and your feet." The next three hours went by quickly as Marielena did these sketches. Margarita sat quietly, moving as directed, and smiling when asked.

With the light starting to fade, Marielena told Margarita that she needed to spend the rest of her time unpacking the canvas and easel. Margarita helped her and soon they had them unpacked and in position for the next day.

Marielena looked at the beautiful tile floor and said, "I'll need a tarpaulin to set under the easel so that I don't drip paint on the tiles. Paint is so difficult to remove if it gets into the grout. It would ruin your beautiful tile floor."

Margarita answered, "I believe that we have some old tarps in the garage. I have to start getting dressed for dinner; but, if you ask Paula, she'll show you out to the garage to get one."

Margarita took Marielena down the back stairs to the kitchen and told Paula what was needed. Paula pointed to the pathway to the garage, explained that the garage wasn't locked, and told Marielena where the tarps were located in the garage.

Margarita asked Marielena, "What time do we start tomorrow?"

Marielena answered, "A las nueve."

Marielena following Paula's directions, went to the garage. In the back of the garage she saw several old tarps. When she looked through them, she saw that one tarp covered an old bicycle that looked in good shape, as far as rideability, but was scratched, dented, and lacked paint in many areas. Some of its parts showed that the original color had been red, but only because a few areas still had paint left between the dents and scrapes. It definitely didn't look like it belonged in the villa or owned by wealthy people. Marielena shrugged, covered it up again, and took one tarpaulin back to the house, up to the second-floor room, and placed it under the newly constructed easel. She sat the canvas on the easel, closed the balcony doors, pulled the drapes, packed her bag, and went downstairs. She intended to leave and return to the village and her apartment.

As she exited through the front door, she met Charles who was returning with the necessary lights. He placed them on the floor of the foyer and asked, "Are you walking down to the village?"

She answered, "Yes, we're finished for the day. I'll be coming back tomorrow at nine. The canvas and easel are in place now; but I'll set up the lights the first thing in the morning, if you can take them upstairs for me now?"

Charles answered, "Yes, I'll carry them upstairs tonight. May I drive you down to the village, you look tired."

Marielena said, "But I thought you and your wife were going out to dinner; she went to dress to go out."

Charles responded, "We are, but it always takes her longer to dress than I take. It will only take a minute or so to drive you down. You understand that I can't do it on a daily basis, but it will give me great pleasure to drive you this first day. Besides I'd like to hear from you about how this first day went."

At that Marielena couldn't refuse, and she was more tired than she had told him.

As they drove down the hill to the village, she told him of the sketches and photos which she had done that day and that all the sketches had gone well. As an afterthought she said that she had gotten a tarpaulin from the garage and put it under the easel and canvas to protect the tile floor.

Charles took a quick breath that startled Marielena; but then he smiled and complimented her on her thoughtfulness to protect the villa's floor.

Marielena insisted that he drop her off and told him to hurry back home. She thanked him for his thoughtfulness in taking her home. As she left the car several of her neighbors saw them laughing together and wondered about why they were together alone.

When Charles arrived home, before he went upstairs to dress for dinner, he went out to the garage to check on his bicycle. It appeared not to have been discovered or moved from where he had hidden it. He berated himself that he had forgotten that she might want a tarpaulin to cover the floor of the "now studio". He was going to have to be more careful. After all, he had a lot to lose if anyone became suspicious of his plans.

CHAPTER 10

THE POLICE COMMISSIONER

CHAPTER 10

THE POLICE COMMISSIONER

Diego Rivera Hernandez Pizzaro Bolivar, a forty-two-year-old police commissioner, sat at his desk and watched the parade of townspeople out the window of his office. He had grown up in this village, a suburb of Toledo, and knew almost everyone who lived here. As with most small towns anywhere in the world, the fascination of village gossips was not only with the people that they had known all their lives, but, especially with anyone new in their village. He had watched Charles Elliot over the four years that he and his wife had resided in their hilltop villa, but today was different. He had never seen Charles with anyone but his wife. Yes, he had also seen him alone, but not with another woman. Today Charles was with someone else who was also new to the village, the young artist from Rhonda.

Diego had seen this artist in the village sketching and doing street painting. Periodically she would sell a sketch or a painting, something neither illegal nor hugely profitable, but he imagined that she was making enough to live on. She had rented the small attic apartment, more like a room, from the Widow Santiago. Perhaps the artist and the widow were both going to be able to live on the little the artist brought in, but he doubted it. Maybe the artist was increasing in income if Charles Elliot was involved; or, the way they were laughing together, it could be something else other than business.

Even though Diego had grown up in this village, Diego had an interesting past elsewhere. Upon graduating from high school, no mean feat for a small-town boy, he had served his country by completing the two-year required military service. It was there that he had elected to become a military policeman. He had liked it enough to pursue being a policeman as a career when he left the service. With recommendations from the military, he went to the police academy in Madrid where he obtained excellent ratings in marksmanship. Upon graduation he applied to the Madrid police force. In the Madrid police force he proved very successful in detective work, solving a cold case murder as well as several others, a case of serial bank robberies, and a series of art forgeries and robberies. Three years after starting this detective job his summer vacation consisted of returning to this, his home village, to help his parents move into a new home. The new home was located across the village from their old one in a new part of town that had just been developed with smaller than average government apartments for the elderly. The first day, not only were his parents moving, but other elderly parents were moving too. One couple was being helped by their daughter, recently graduated from the university in Salamanca. As usual with elderly people, who begin in new surroundings, the two elderly couples got acquainted, and he became acquainted with the daughter. That was the first of many trips home to see his parents and their friend's daughter, Amaya.

The two young people discovered that they had much in common; and, with both set of parents' blessings, they married the following summer. Amaya joined Diego in Madrid, but both worried about their elderly parents and wished to be near them. So, five years later, when an opening for police commissioner became available in the village, they left Madrid so that Diego could become the commissioner in his old hometown. While it was a step up in one way, it was a step backward in another. Diego got a healthy raise in pay and they were near both their parents, but the excitement of the large city police force was missing, as well as the many varied crime-solving opportunities. The village had a history of few crimes and the police force was small.

They had only been back in the village permanently for a year when Amaya was diagnosed with colon cancer. Despite radiation and chemotherapy, she continued to decline, getting weaker and weaker. The elderly parents, whom they had come back to care for in their later years, saw instead their daughter and daughter-in-law predecease them. It was one of the saddest funerals seen in the village for many years. Diego was heartbroken, and although he had wanted to return to his police duties left behind in Madrid, he didn't feel that he could in good conscience leave behind the two sets of elderly parents. He stayed in the small village with little crime as its police commissioner while he was filled with memories of his much beloved wife.

Diego's wife had now been dead two years; and, although he hated being unmarried and was very lonesome at times, there was no one whom he knew that could ever fill his heart as Amaya had. The young artist had seemed nice, when he had made her acquaintance; and, he had thought about asking her out, but she was probably too young for him. Too bad, maybe she was involved with Charles Elliot who had the beautiful ex-Miss World for a wife. He hoped not. There had been rumors that Charles had been and might still be something other than the devoted husband he wanted to seem like. Most of those rumors had been spawned by tabloid photos and stories from different places other than in his village. Diego knew that the Elliot family was supposed to be landed and wealthy Brits, who had business dealings all over the world. Everyone knew that Charles had wooed the Spanish Miss World and won her away from her people.

Diego had tried not to be an extremely biased person all his life, but he always felt that Margarita would have done better marrying someone from her own Spanish people and background. But who was he to judge? Diego's family had also been poor, just like Margarita's family. Perhaps Margarita had married for money. He realized just how wealth could be an incentive for people to do strange things, even marry someone who maybe shouldn't even be dated, He knew about Margarita Elliot's family background in Mallorca; how she had championed the poor, illiterate and underfed children in her reign as Miss World; and how she had helped her parents and the Balearic Islands. He admired how even though she was now wealthy, Margarita worked with the church's young people. Padre Juan, when he wasn't tending to the church's duties, would sometimes come into his office to talk and share a cup of coffee. Such visits had started when he was trying to confront the sorrow of losing his wife, but the two had become close friends over the years. Padre Juan stated that Margarita was a genuinely sweet and caring individual who was a great asset in caring for the church's young people, especially the young children.

Hearing a knock on the door, he was delighted to see that the person in his thoughts, Padre Juan, was again at his door. As they conversed, he mentioned to the holy father that he had seen Charles in the village with the young artist, Marielena. While he had casually brought this sighting up, the Padre looked up quickly at him and then stated that some of his other parishioners had told him that they also had seen them together. He himself had seen them together sitting at the local café with their heads together in deep discussion. After the priest had left, Diego mused about these new bits of information. Something was going on with the artist and Charles, and it didn't look good if people were talking about them.

THE PAINTING

CHAPTER 11

THE PAINTING

Charles decided that it was time to obtain all of the necessary props for the stage of his crime. Charles told Margarita that he would have to leave for Italy on a business trip on Thursday morning. He said that he had hoped not to be taking any trips during the painting of the portrait; however, one of his business associates was having a problem which, unfortunately, he needed to help with. He promised to be gone only a few days and would be in touch with her by phone if she needed anything. He told her that he would be bringing her gifts. He asked if she had any problem being alone in the house with the artist and their staff.

"Oh no, darling," she responded.

Charles did indeed go to Italy for business ... the business of getting rid of Margarita. As he was leaving for Italy, he telephoned Lady Louise in England to arrange a little "side business" on his Italy trip. When he reached Italy, he first went to see his old Mafia friends who had secured four different blank passports, associated credit and business cards, and four different disguises. The disguises were comprised of wigs with different hair colors, different glasses, a beard, a goatee, a mustache, and different jackets, shirts, and sweaters. The wigs were accompanied by skull caps to go underneath so that the wigs would remain attached to his head and not slip off or to one side. The price was extremely high, but Charles paid the bill without any complaint. He reminded his associates that he was doubling the amount they had requested as he wrote the check because he was not only purchasing all the items, but he was also buying their silence.

Donning each of the four disguises in turn, he was photographed for the four passports. The photos were then expertly inserted into their proper blank passports. The job was done so well that, unless you looked under a microscope, you would never realize they had been doctored. Since he had convinced Lady Louise to make a quick trip to Italy and she had also arranged to conduct business while in Italy, she was busy with her business meetings at the same time that he was tending to the "business" with his Mafia friends. He had lied to her saying that he was on family business, not that his business was to arrange to kill his wife. The evenings and nights they were together and enjoyed each other to the fullest. Again, as with his entire life, he was leading two separate lives. When the five days which they spent together were over, he vowed to her that they would be together soon and that he loved her very much. As they parted, he thought about how wonderful a permanent union with her would be.

Charles, instead of returning to Spain immediately, went shopping. He went to an exclusive jewelry store in Rome and purchased a stunning gold bracelet with garnets for Margarita. He believed that it would match the necklace and earrings which he had previously given her. She would be overwhelmed that he had been thinking of her on a business trip. On one of his trips to Madrid he had ordered a garnet-colored silk dress from a very prestigious seamstress to match the garnet color of the jewelry.

The next day on the way home he stopped at the seamstress's in Madrid and picked up the dress. Upon arriving home, Charles entered the house carrying the huge box from the seamstress and a smaller one which he presented to Margarita.

"Oh, what are these?" Margarita asked.

"Remember that I promised you presents when I came home from Italy? Please, open them first and then I'll explain," was Charles's answer.

Margarita opened the small box first and exclaimed, "Oh you sweet thing, it matches the necklace and earrings which you gave me. What a lovely surprise!" Then she opened the large box and said as she held the garnet bracelet next to the gown, "Is this to wear with the jewelry ... they match perfectly."

Charles then said, "Yes, these are early birthday presents so that you can be painted in them."

"Oh, I love it all," as she kissed him. "But, most of all, I love you."

Charles thought to himself, now if I can get the rest of my plans to go as smoothly, I'll be the one who's really happy.

The next morning, again using business as an excuse, Charles went back to Madrid. This time he stopped along the highway to put on one of the disguises. He went into an antiques store that carried Toledo steel objects. He found what he was looking for, an antique Toledo dagger which was much in need of sharpening. It was expensive, but he believed that it would suit his purposes. He removed the disguise as he left Madrid, drove home, and, seeing that Margarita was occupied with sitting for her portrait, he took the knife and hid it in a small chest in one of the many guest rooms in the villa. That evening at dinner, he complained to Isa, the cook, that his steak knife was so dull he could hardly cut his meat. He asked when the knives and scissors in the house had last been sharpened.

Isa replied, "Last year, Señor."

He said then, "I think every knife and scissors in the house should be sharpened." After dinner, when Margarita had gone upstairs to change into her nightclothes, he called Paula, the housekeeper, and said to her," I have decided that every knife and scissors in the house should be sharpened. Isa has said that it has been a year since they were last sharpened. Please see about this matter for me. He then instructed Paula to find "an old knife stored in a chest in the guest bedroom closet. "I believe this knife belonged to Margarita's grandfather; and, perhaps for sentimental reasons, it should be included in her portrait that the artist is working on."

The next morning Paula and Isa worked together to gather all the utensils needing sharpening and listened for the scissor grinder to come through the village. As expected, he did work his way through the village and ended up near the villa. Paula rushed out to apprehend him in the street and watched him patiently as each item, including the beautiful antique dagger, was sharpened. It took the scissor grinder almost two hours to sharpen every utensil that they had brought out to him. Both the cook and the housekeeper knew that Charles would be happy, especially with the sheen and sharpness of Margarita's grandfather's dagger. The grinder had done a wonderful job with it. It almost looked new.

Later that day, Charles worked with Paula and Isa on finding the correct bowl, candlesticks, goblets, cheese board, bread board, and wine decanter for the table. The women dearly loved Margarita and were delighted to be included in the selection of the props to be in the portrait. Isa promised to keep the fruit bowl, and cheese and bread boards filled daily as needed for the portrait sittings. Paula had the drapes taken down, dusted, and returned to the room so that the artist would see them in immaculate condition and paint them with their lush colors showing.

The following day was the fifth day of portrait setting and Marielena arrived promptly at nine to begin her day's work. Margarita and Charles met her together and Charles put the various items on the table to complete the still-life portion of the portrait's background. Charles had just come in from an early meeting in Madrid and hadn't removed his driving gloves; therefore, his fingerprints weren't on any of the items which had been cleaned thoroughly by Isa and Paula.

Feigning ignorance, he condescendingly stated, "Marielena, as you're the artist here and, I'm sure you've set up many still-life objects for paintings, we're going to leave it up to you to do the table setting in an artistic way. Once you have it arranged, other than refilling the fruit bowl and cheese and bread boards, we and our staff won't touch anything on the table again. We feel comfortable with whatever arrangement you come up with." Then he smiled broadly at Marielena and Margarita. His wife quickly agreed with his decision. While she hadn't been consulted prior to this, she could see the good reasoning behind his words. They both stood back and let Marielena arrange and continue rearranging the items until she was totally satisfied with the effect.

One thought came to her as she was moving the items around, sometimes only fractions of centimeters; however, she said nothing. She wondered why there wasn't a bread or paring knife along with the food. I seemed odd that there was only a dagger. While the villa was close to Toledo, known for its swords, daggers, battle axes, and ceremonial knives, why had Charles and Margarita chosen a dagger as the knife to be on the table? It looked like it had been recently sharpened, and she tried not to touch the blade.

Margarita excused herself, stating that she needed to see Isa for a few minutes to plan a light lunch for them. As she left the room, Marielena asked Charles about the dagger.

Smiling, he explained that the dagger had been Margarita's grandfather's and it was being included in the portrait for sentimental reasons.

Well, she thought, that explains it, and dismissed the questionable nature of the dagger from her mind.

Charles then, removing his driving gloves, excused himself, with "I'm sure Margarita will return shortly. I'll leave so you can get started working today." As Charles left the room, he hoped that Marielena wouldn't say anything about his fictitious history of the dagger.

It wasn't but a few moments, long enough for Marielena to squeeze some fresh paint onto her palette, straighten the canvas on the easel, and consult her sketches that Margarita reentered the room bearing a pitcher of cold lemonade.

"Isa will be coming up with some sandwiches around two, but I thought we could use a cool drink now."

"That's very kind of you."

Chapter 11 - The Painting

"Where would you like me to be today?" Margarita asked.

"I think I'd like to block in your position near the table, and then you can do whatever you wish for the rest of the morning as I can work on the still-life portion of the painting now that all the objects are here. I think that I can have that finished and begin work on the background window, doors, drapes, and garden tomorrow morning when it's cool enough to open the doors the way you and Charles want them painted."

Margarita responded, "That sounds like a good plan, and that way I can perhaps go down to the library today and then stop at the church and see the children there. I haven't had a chance to go there for a few days."

Marielena continued, "I'm aware that time is limited and, with the days beginning to get hotter in the afternoons, perhaps I can spend the mornings completing that part of the canvas, and spend the afternoons concentrating on you, your gown, and jewelry. One thing though," she paused, "I would like you to leave your gown here in this room all the time, because I need to match the color of the garden flowers outside to your gown color. To have a cohesive painting, colors need to be placed all around the canvas so that the eye moves through a painting. I could also add some color reflections in the carpet and draperies."

"Of course, "Margarita answered. "I'll go about my other duties this morning and also write a nice letter to my family in Mallorca. I'll check back with you around two when Isa should have our lunch ready." She smiled and then exited the room.

Marielena thought hard about Margarita's background. From what little she had heard from her in their first conversation about the poorness of her family, she again wondered how Margarita's grandfather had owned such an expensive dagger from Toledo? She made up her mind to ask Margarita about it another day.

CHAPTER 12

THE PORTRAIT CONTINUES

CHAPTER 12

THE PORTRAIT CONTINUES

Every day followed the same course. Marielena would rise at sunrise, dress, eat a quick breakfast, and walk to the villa. Mornings were spent on the canvas's background, and afternoons she worked on sketching Margarita, at least in pieces of separate paper. By the end of two weeks, the still-life of the bowl, bread and cheese boards, cheese, bread, goblets, dagger, and candlesticks was completed. The window, doors, drapes, small rug, and tiles were almost finished. The garden beyond was finished in a semi-reduced manner because of distance and the fact that Margarita was the main part of the canvas. The garden was more or less impressionistic compared to the interior and the focus of the portrait. All that remained to be finished was Margarita herself. Marielena had been careful to leave a blank area on the canvas, except for a sketchy outline over a warm rosy base coat, where she would place Margarita. She would use her detailed sketches, as well as Margarita in the standing pose, to fill in that area to finish the portrait.

Periodically Charles would check in to the painting studio room to see how she was progressing. She was happy to see that, so far, he approved of the portrait. What began to bother her, however, was that Charles also stopped by, always unannounced, at her attic apartment. These visits were also accompanied by strange, and also hostile, looks from her landlady and some of her close neighbors who knew who Charles was and what his marital status was. Marielena had told Señora Santiago that she was painting a portrait of Margarita, but her disapproving looks were still disconcerting. She had told Señora Santiago about her commission when she had paid her rent in advance out of the down payment monies for the portrait. She thought, had she not told her, it would have made her very nervous to have her landlady see her with a married man. The moral attitudes of Spanish society were very set as to what unmarried young women were allowed to do. Her landlady might even ask her to vacate her room, even though she knew Señora Santiago needed the income from her rent. Nonetheless, it made her anxious to have him "just show up". She had experienced a lot of difficulty finding an apartment that she could afford, and she couldn't bear to lose this one.

Today, as she reported to the villa, Margarita met her and inquired about the day's schedule. Margarita knew that Marielena had everything in the portrait done, except herself.

Marielena answered her query with, "I'd like to start with your body in it's gown. You can leave the jewelry off today, but we'll have to start two hour sitting sessions interspersed with an hour rest. And, I'm afraid, with the time constraints, we'll have to do this every day until the portrait is completed."

"I only need to do one thing this morning," said Margarita. I need to go to the library; but that won't take long."

"OK," said Marielena, "that will give me time to start mixing my paints on my pallet. I need to match skin tones and dress tones."

Both women proceeded to carry out their plans before continuing the painting.

Margarita hadn't been to the library for two weeks. She had wanted to go several days earlier, but when she had gone to the church, she had been so happy to see all the children, that she had spent too much time there and hadn't gotten to the library. Charles had taken two trips during that two-week time period, once to England and once to Italy. She visited the newspaper and tabloid section of the library, searched the issues of the dates needed, and, sure enough, she had her answers. In the tabloids under the gossip sections was a photo of Charles with the same woman again. She couldn't understand. He was continually proclaiming his devotion to her while in her presence. Margarita photocopied the pages as she had done before. She added the dates and times to the records that she was keeping in her journal. As she returned and entered the villa, Charles was leaving and gave her an ardent kiss. Returning the kiss, she thought, "if he can lead some sort of a double life, so can I."

She went to her room where she had stored all the previous photocopies of articles and photos, collected them, and entered the studio room where Marielena was ready to begin work. Standing there in the entry, looking at her gown hanging there ready to be put on for the setting, she suddenly felt absolutely helpless.

Marielena looked up and, recognizing by Margarita's facial expression and body language that something was wrong, rushed to her side. "Oh, Margarita, what in the world is wrong? You look totally lost."

With that, Margarita sobbed and said, "I have no one to share this with. I can't tell my parents, and I have no friends in the village. I have acquaintances, but no friend to whom I can tell secrets. And - I don't know what to do or whom to turn to."

She then showed the photocopies of photos, photocopies of tabloid and newspaper articles, and her journal entries of Charles's business trip dates compared to the dates of her photocopied items. She explained to Marielena how she had inadvertently come across all the information which she had collected concerning Charles and, at first other women, now 'other woman'.

Marielena looked at the photos, counted them, and saw by the dates in the journal that at least this current affair had progressed over some time. She asked, "Does Charles know of your suspicions?"

"No, but I've spoken to Padre Juan in Confession and also to Pastor Luis at the church on Calle Judit. They are the only ones who know. Now you know. What am I to do? Padre Juan said to pray. Pastor Luis said to wait and see if what I suspected continued. I'm beginning to be afraid to leave these documents in the house for fear Charles will find them."

Marielena thought for a moment. "I can take them with me and hide them in my apartment for you, at least while I am coming and going from here. What else did the padre and pastor tell you to do?"

"Continue as though nothing has happened, continue collecting photos and dates, and pretend that all is well. That is getting more and more difficult for me to do." At that Margarita broke down in fresh tears. She continued, "What would you suggest I do?"

Marielena frowned and said, "I think that I'd do as they suggest, which means we need to continue with this portrait and wait. I'll think about your problem, hide these documents, and we'll act as normal as we can."

Margarita nodded her head slowly and tried to dry her eyes.

Marielena continued, "If we stop doing the portrait, Charles will suspect that something is wrong."

Margarita left the room, went into her bathroom, and washed her face. She came back in her usual composed way, put on the beautiful garnet-colored gown, and stood in her appointed spot by the table under the window. She looked absolutely beautiful, but Marielena thought that her facial expression, instead of looking radiantly happy, more resembled Leonardo's "Mona Lisa" and the almost imperceptible wistfulness of a smile. As Marielena looked at the scene before her, her eyes wandered to the table behind Margarita and its many objects already painted into the portrait's background. Her eyes rested on the dagger, and her previously unasked question about its origin came to mind. Now, in light of the information which Margarita had shared with her, it seemed important to her to ask her question.

"Margarita, the dagger on the table is beautiful and looks

very old. Such daggers, made obviously in Toledo, are horribly expensive. Charles told me that it was your grandfather's. Did you give it to Charles? Or do you know anything about how it was obtained? I know you came from a poor family, like I did."

Margarita looked directly at Marielena and, with a shocked expression on her face, she said, "I don't know anything about the dagger. It wasn't owned by my grandfather. He was a poor shepherd with barely enough money to feed his family. What little he had, such as family heirlooms, he had to sell during the Civil War in order to have money to survive. I have no idea why Charles would say such a thing. What a curious thing for him to say."

Marielena asked again, "So you have no idea where it came from?"

"No," replied Margarita, "no idea."

"Why do you think Charles told me that story?"

"I don't know, but I never laid eyes on that dagger until Charles told Paula to add it to the group of items that he wanted on the table here," Margarita said pointing to the table.

"Strange," Marielena said. "Oh well, let's get started again," as she picked up her pallet and brush.

The rest of the morning and afternoon they worked at the portrait until late in the end of the day when they bade each other goodbye with Margarita retreating into the interior of the villa and Marielena leaving the villa with Margarita's "evidence" tucked deeply into the bottom of her rucksack of artist supplies. When she reached her apartment, she took the documents and hid them in the bottom of her armoire for safe keeping.

The next three days were the same for the two women. Two hours of portrait setting with one hour of rest between continued. Some of the breaks were accompanied by cold drinks, some with lunch, and some with snacks to keep Margarita and Marielena's strength restored to continue with the sittings. They never mentioned the documents again, but both of them could think of nothing else. Margarita thought of them with the reassurance that her friend would keep them safe and away from Charles, and Marielena thought of them as an unusual storage of Charles's infidelity and Margarita's deep trust in her and the friendship between them.

CHAPTER 13

BUSY CHARLES

CHAPTER 13

BUSY CHARLES

During the time that Margarita was posing for her portrait and Marielena was engrossed in doing the best painting of her life, Charles became aware that the portrait was almost finished. He needed to add fuel to the fire that would scorch Marielena. Charles must make sure that Marielena would be accused of performing the murder of Margarita. He needed to plan exactly when he would commit the murder. Furthermore, he needed to plan for the unveiling ceremony of the portrait and Margarita's birthday; and he needed to make it appear as though they would really take place. He knew they wouldn't, but, if he acted like they wouldn't take place, he would be the suspect, not Marielena.

The first step was to make sure that Marielena would be at the scene of the crime, permanently. The following morning when the women were in the studio, he went into the room. He said that with Margarita's birthday quickly approaching and time being of the essence, he had thought of a way by which he could speed up the painting process. The women looked at him and inquired how. He said that the villa had many unused guest rooms. As he phrased the next part, he gave neither of the women any excuse to say "no" to his proposal. "I think that until the portrait is finished, Marielena should move into the villa, so that she doesn't have to commute back and forth to the village every day. She is wasting energy and time doing that. I don't know why I didn't think of this sooner, but now that I have, what do you think, Margarita?"

Of course, Margarita was delighted with the idea. She would now have her friend, the artist, in the house with her at all times. Even though Charles didn't know why she was happy about the idea, he knew that he had pulled off another of his plans. He stated that he would be happy to come get Marielena the next morning and move her into the villa before she started work.

The second step was to plan the ceremony. What date and time; who would attend because invitations would have to be printed and sent out; what would be served so that the ordering of wines, food, serving people hired, and clean up people hired? Looking at the calendar marked with the date of Margarita's birthday, he sat down the same evening, after Marielena had gone home, with Margarita and they discussed all the items on his list. He thought it would be a nice touch to have prepared a written list to consult with her so that she would decide that he was really engrossed in making preparations for her birthday and that she would feel that he loved her enough to include her wishes in the preparation of the celebration. He decided that it would be wise to include her in his choices of day, time, and food to order because, after all, she was the lady of the villa. If she were involved, she would really believe that this was to be a true celebration and would prove his love to her. Of course, among all the attendees would be all her family, his family, all the dignitaries in their village, including the police commissioner, many of his business associates in Spain, and maybe a few business associates from England, France, Italy, Germany, and India. All in all, the total number of invitations approached five hundred. That number of individuals would be no problem in terms of space as the villa was large and tents could be erected on the lawn and gardens. Tables and chairs could be rented. He and Margarita drew up plans for the menu, which they then discussed with Paula and Isa. Between the four of them, they concluded planning the number of extra servers and clean up people that would need to be hired for such a huge party. They made a list of service agencies where the extra people would be hired and how much they were willing to pay them, adding generous tips. With so many people attending, there would be an enormous number of cars that would clog the road to the villa. Additional parking would be required most likely off site with some sort of shuttle service provided. He knew that the narrow roads up to the villa would never provide enough parking.

Even the extra servers and cleanup crew would require parking.

The third step was to involve the police - after all he was a law-abiding citizen planning a huge party. Under the pretext that he was inviting the police commissioner to the celebration, he went into the village to speak with him. He told the commissioner about his plans for the celebration and the unveiling of Margarita's portrait as a huge birthday celebration for his wife. He asked the commissioner to attend the celebration and also to help plan for the traffic congestion with all the extra cars of the visitors and hired help. The commissioner suggested using the village's parking lots near the train station as designated parking for all the guests and hired help. That area would also be available for anyone coming via train. Shuttles would then run between those parking areas and the villa on an hourly basis. Charles would also need to arrange for shuttle buses and drivers. As they spoke, Charles thanked Commissioner Rivera profusely for his suggestions and said that he would put directions in the invitations indicating where attendees could park and how they could board the shuttle buses to the villa. He again urged the commissioner to attend the fete himself.

During his discussion with Commissioner Rivera, he casually let drop that in spite of his marriage, he had become very good friends with the portrait artist, Marielena. He assumed that their friendship had probably been a good thing, since she had worked very hard to please him with a wonderful portrait of his wife; but recently he had been bothered when Marielena had dropped several hints to him that she considered him more than a friend. She said that she was falling in love with him. If fact, as he had that very morning moved her into the villa these last weeks to finish the portrait, she had said, "I love you", to him. He stated, "I will be glad when the portrait is finished, so that she will be moving out."

While Commissioned Rivera didn't respond in any way to this revelation, he added the information to his previously-formed suspicions concerning the relationship between Charles and Marielena. He hoped that he had maintained a poker face throughout his conversation. After Charles had left, he tried to speculate as to a reason for Charles "letting it slip" about Marielena's feelings for him. He appreciated being asked to the celebration and being appraised as to the traffic problems during the celebration as they were realistic concerns for the police force. He was happy that he had proposed the parking lots and shuttle buses. They would prevent the congestion to the village streets with the number of cars involved.

When Charles had moved Marielena into the villa that morning, he did two things. First, he made sure that all her neighbors watched him carry out her bags and deposit them in his car. The villagers needed to know that she was going away, in some kind of respect, with him. Second, he chose a guest room in the villa which was furthest away from the studio. He didn't want her to be anywhere near the studio on the night when he would commit the murder. She should not be able to see or hear anything occurring there. He stated to her that he thought she would rest better in the room which faced east, not west. She would not be bothered after a long day painting by a sunset, and she would be awakened early in the morning to begin her painting day.

His fourth step was to order the invitations and send them out. He ordered the printing with an additional sheet of paper in each invitation describing the location of parking and the existence of a shuttle bus from the parking lots to the villa. He even showed them to Margarita to get her approval. He laughed to himself as he placed the order for the food and wines and for the hired help at the Toledo agency for service employees. He alone knew that the last two orders would be cancelled with regret. He worked with Paula addressing all the invitations before they were sent out. While it seemed a waste of good time and money, it was all a convincing front for a celebration which would never happen. Always two sides ... one transparent, one opaque.

His fifth step was to start looking at weather forecasts. Two weeks after Marielena was ensconced in the villa and the painting was almost finished, he learned that in three days there would be a large cold front with severe thunderstorms sweeping over Spain, with even possible thunderstorms and waterspouts. While proceeding with his plans for the celebration, making sure that the invitations had arrived and had been sent out, he spoke to Marielena to ensure that the portrait would be finished on time. At the last minute that day, he faked an overseas call to himself. He then informed Margarita that, unfortunately, he needed to go to England on family business for the next four days. He packed his suitcase and purchased round trip airline tickets for a direct flight to England from Madrid. All was ready as he left the next morning.

CHAPTER 14

THE FOUL DEED

CHAPTER 14

THE FOUL DEED

Instead of Charles going to his London apartment when he reached England, he went to his parent's manor on the pretext that he wanted to check up on them, especially his father. He had recently been busy and hadn't seen them for a while. Both parents were delighted. Later, still using the excuse of family business, he went into London for several hours to his company office. He thought that he was covering all his bases and establishing his perfect alibi. While in the office he, indeed, carried out several important transactions to further the alibi, including calling all section heads for a strategy meeting covering the next six months of business ventures. He asked that the section heads write up reports on all their major operations. He also made arrangements to go to India and Japan in the next month, following his wife's birthday celebration. After all he couldn't go during that "special time" he explained to everyone. He made sure to call Lady Louise and explain that, while he would miss her terribly, he would not be able to spend time with her for a month, maybe two months. He was going to be tied up with so many business meetings that he wouldn't have any spare time. He assumed that would keep her from trying to reach him; and, if she did try to reach him and was unable to touch base with him, she would conclude that he was traveling or in meetings. He hoped that prevented him from awkwardly trying to explain where he was and what he was doing.

The next day he again went to the office, but he locked himself in his office and very carefully packed his backpack. He verified that he had all four disguises, passports, credit cards, rubber gloves, plastic jumpsuit, shoe covers, sanitary wipes, paper towels, and extra plastic garbage bags. Everything that he thought he might need in the next couple of days. He smiled with the realization that he didn't need a murder weapon. It was already on site. He had brought the backpack folded up in his briefcase. As he left the office, he carried both his briefcase and the backpack down the back staircase to the underground garage. As he had left the office later than almost all the employees, he thought he had reached his car unseen by anyone. Unfortunately for him, he had forgotten about the security cameras in the company garage.

As he entered his parent's house that evening, he complained to his mother that he had a headache and felt like he might be coming down with something. He made the same complaint as he entered the kitchen and asked the cook for some hot tea and toast. Inwardly he was laughing as he thought of the food which he had already consumed before coming home and the extra food which he had stored in his briefcase for the next day.

The following morning, after consulting the weather reports, he continued to complain about how badly he felt. At last in the afternoon, with a huge sigh, he told everyone that he was going to take some sleeping pills, go to bed early, and try to "sleep off" whatever it was that he had picked up. He requested that he not be disturbed. He would come downstairs whenever he felt like it, so "just let me sleep". He added for good measure, "I'm afraid that whatever I've got, I'll give to my dad who has enough health problems as it is." He thought that added a nice touch to his story. Both parents were extremely sympathetic and seemed relieved that he was being so considerate.

He had stored his backpack in the garage when he had come in from the office, except for one disguise which he had put in his briefcase. Extinguishing all the lights in his room, he put on that disguise as it was starting to become dusk outside. He opened his bedroom window, climbed out the window, and leaving a small crack in the bottom, he climbed out and down the vines that grew there. Keeping to the lengthening shadows, he ran across the yard to the garage. He knew his parents were in the dining room having dinner at this particular time and wouldn't be watching the yard. On the contrary, his mother had just gotten up to shut the dining room shutters and noted some movement down on the lawn. Looking more closely, she realized that, although the size and shape of the person she saw resembled her son, the appearance was different. She assumed that a stranger had gotten into their yard and called the gardener to go check. By the time the gardener reached the spot where she had described seeing someone, Charles was long gone, having gone through the garage, picking up the backpack, and walking quickly to the woods a quarter kilometer up the road where he had hidden a rental car which he had obtained in one of his disguises. Even if it were found eventually, it could not be traced to him. He made a hasty escape toward London.

In London he put the car in a long-term parking lot, went to the train station, and purchased a ticket for a sleeping car on the fast train to Paris, his first leg of his journey. In Paris, he changed to a fast train to Madrid; and, arriving in Madrid, he rode the last bus to Toledo. It was well past midnight and starting to rain by the time he reached Toledo. Not only were the streets dark, but they were deserted. It was not a night when people would want to be abroad. He walked from Toledo to the village and then to the villa. As in Toledo, there was no one on the streets. In the distance to the northwest he could see that the gentle rain, which had covered his progress from Toledo, was now developing into the forecasted, horrible, thunderstorm. The weathermen had gotten it correct this time.

He slipped through the back door of the villa's garage from the alley, rolled the bicycle from its hiding place, and set it under some bushes next to the back gate. The ground was soft and the tires made tracks in the soft ground under the bush, but it was so dark that he couldn't see them. He assumed that whatever rain was going to come down would cover any tracks that the bicycle made. Moving quickly through the dark, he put on a mask, rubber gloves and his plastic jumpsuit, which had extra rubber gloves, a garbage bag, and wipes in the pocket. Leaving his backpack in the garage, he went to the servants' entrance to the kitchen. At this time of night there were no lights anywhere. He moved through the kitchen to the servants' back stairs and went up to the room that was being used as a studio. He waited until the storm broke and then turned on the lights, pushed back the draperies, and opened the balcony doors. The lights from the room fell on the balcony and outside staircase. The storm howled overhead. He knew that from his and Margarita's bedroom, the window and balcony doors of the studio were visible. Margarita, who couldn't sleep during bad thunderstorms, would get up, look out, and see the lights on in the studio.

He waited until he saw the light go on in their bedroom, counted down slowly, turned off the lights in the studio room, partly closed the drapes, and picked up the dagger from the table. The wind and water were now coming in through the open balcony doors and the partly closed drapes. The room was now dark, he was dressed all in black, and the heavy draperies were blocking most of the light from the lightning. He was sure that, whenever Margarita entered the room, he would not be seen. He waited. As he did, the rain, which was falling heavily and coming though the studio door, was being blown across the tile floor and was collecting in puddles.

Suddenly, as the thunder rolled and a huge thunderbolt streaked across the sky, Margarita entered the studio.

As she entered and ran toward the open door, she exclaimed, "How did the doors come open? Oh, what a mess!"

At that moment Charles sprang from the concealment of the drapes and, with one hand firmly clamping his wife's mouth shut, he slashed her throat. No sound had escaped. Blood spurted onto the floor mingling with all the rainwater. Charles felt an almost animal glee at seeing his dying wife; but, just to be sure, he continued stabbing her until she was sagging in his arms. She was dead. He let her drop to the floor and threw the dagger down beside her.

He had planned carefully. From the pocket of the plastic

jumpsuit, he extracted a huge garbage bag into which he put his mask, his shoe covers, and the plastic jumpsuit. Standing totally nude, except for his rubber gloves, he shut the drapes over the balcony doors which were still open. He slithered through the drapery opening onto the balcony and down the stairs carrying his shoes. At the bottom of the stairs was a huge downspout from which gushed a torrent of rainwater. Charles stood under it to make sure that all his body, head, feet, and hands were thoroughly washed and whatever blood had happened to get on him was washed away into the garden. Running quickly to the garage, he at last removed the rubber gloves and added them to the garbage bag. He went to the backpack, removed his clothes of the next disguise putting them on as well as his shoes, and left the garage the same way that he had entered. He went to the bicycle and pushed it out of the gate into the alleyway, closing the gate behind him with his elbow. Riding the bike down to the bridge over the river on the way to the train station, he threw both the garbage bag and the bicycle into the river. The river was approaching flood stage with all the rainfall. He assumed the bag would never be found, but there wasn't any connection between him and the bicycle, even if it was found. Looking around he saw no one. Good! Glancing at his watch, he realized that the first train to Madrid from Toledo was going to leave in an hour. He walked quickly from his small village to Toledo and purchased a ticket from the vending machine, being sure that he had used another pair of rubber-gloves to avoid leaving any fingerprints.

As the train left the Toledo station, he sighed with relief. There weren't but a few passengers and no one seemed to take notice of him. Even though he knew that he was in disguise, he had visions of someone asking him a question or making a comment to which he would have to answer. With the early hour he assumed that everyone was too concerned with their own thoughts to bother him. That was a good thing.

All went well and soon he was in the rail station at Madrid. He went into the men's bathroom and changed into the third disguise. It was fortunate that it was so early since there was no one in the restroom. He had a small sack that he had put the clothes from his last disguise in. He couldn't bring himself to throw away the passport and business cards of the disguise. He had gone to too much trouble to get them and he might need them sometime in the future. He put them back into his backpack, but he put the facial parts of his disguise into a different plastic bag. If in the future, he needed those facial parts, he could always obtain them. As he moved through the terminal, he disposed of those parts of his disguise piece by piece as he came to different trash cans. By the time he purchased his ticket on the fast train to Paris, he had only one more disguise which he would use in Paris. He had purchased a sleeping car ticket to Paris, so that he grabbed a few winks of sleep on the way to Paris. When he arrived in Paris, he repeated the same procedure as in Madrid.

By the time he purchased his ticket to London, he again had a sleeping compartment with a locked compartment door. He breathed a huge sigh of relief, and again slept. A huge burden had been lifted from his mind. There was also a huge burden from his life that had been removed.

As the train approached London, his wrist alarm went off. He rose from the bunk, looked around at everything, took out wipes, and tried to remember everything that he had touched. He wiped down everything thoroughly. He had just finished when the train pulled in. He took one more wipe and used it on the door handles, in and out. He joined the people queueing up to exit.

He exited the train and again went into the men's water closet. He removed his last disguise, knowing that he probably wouldn't see anyone in the station that he knew. But, if he did, he would be himself and not be in a disguise. He wondered if he should ditch this last disguise but decided that this time he would simply put it into his backpack. It had served him well and was the last of his disguises. He mused that maybe he might like to use it again. Leaving the station, he walked to the long-term parking lot, poked his exit ticket into the machine, and drove to the woods near the manor where he again wiped everything down that he had touched. He walked back to the alley behind the manor's garage and on the way, he disposed of all the wipes, putting some under rotting leaves, some in a neighbor's trash bin, and some in his own trash bin.

Somehow, he managed to slip in through the servant's quarters, upstairs, out a window into the ivy, over the ivy to his own window, and, sliding his window up, entered his own room. He made his bed appear to have been slept in, poured the water and pills from his nightstand down the toilet, and turned his shower on. His backpack with the last disguise still left, passports, credit cards, business cards, and all his clothing which remained, he pushed far back into his closet. He would have to get rid of at least the clothing later, but he didn't have time now. As he thought though, they might come in handy at a later time. He just didn't seem able to contemplate getting rid of them when they had worked so nicely for him.

With having a shower and putting on clean clothes, he emerged, went downstairs, kissed his mother, and told her that he was so glad that he had taken the medicine and sleeping pills the night before. He had slept like a log and was now feeling so much better. And he looked better too. With the naps between Madrid and Paris, and between Paris and London, he had been refreshed. Now all he had to do was wait.

CHAPTER 15

THE DISCOVERY

CHAPTER 15

THE DISCOVERY

Meanwhile in Spain Marielena had not slept well during all the storms that night and was late rising. Looking at her watch she realized that she would be late reaching the studio this morning. Maybe it was a good thing that Margarita and Charles had insisted she stay at the villa until the portrait was completed. She rose quickly, dressed, and without making her bed or going into the kitchen for food, she rushed to the studio to get started preparing her palette for the day's painting. She was happy that the painting was finished except for a few minor touches.

As she entered the studio, she noticed a strange smell; and, realizing that the curtains needed to be drawn back, she ran to open them. She became aware that the floor was wet only as her feet started to slip. And, as she started to fall down, she spotted something lying in her way. It was the body of Margarita. Marielena was now wet, not only by the water puddled on the floor, but also blood. As she hit the floor, she screamed. It was a piercing scream that echoed throughout the studio and also throughout the villa. Lying there beside the body was the dagger. The dagger which she had questioned and which should have been on the table beside the window. The dagger which was part of the portrait that she had been working on. The dagger which, obviously, had been used to kill her friend, Margarita.

Her scream brought Isa and Paula running from the rest of the house. Even the gardener looked up at the upstairs windows and hurried up the balcony stairs. He had gone out that morning to see if there had been any damage to the yard, gardens, or house during the night's storms. Arriving at the same time, all three of the staff stared at Marielena who was covered in blood and lying next to Margarita and the dagger.

Chapter 15 - The Discovery

They all jumped to the same conclusion - it had been Margarita who had screamed as Marielena killed her. They also assumed that the reason for all the blood covering both women and the floor was that there had been a struggle between them resulting in the murder. If Margarita had been killed earlier, the blood would have coagulated and been thicker. Margarita was recently killed; therefore, this blood was fresh blood which the water was diluting.

The gardener and one woman, Paula, grabbed Marielena, while the other, Isa, rushed to the phone and called the police commissioner. The more Marielena protested and tried to pull away, the harder they held her. There was no way they were going to let the murderer of their mistress get away. Furthermore, with Marielena being covered in so much blood, she had to have been in the process of killing Margarita.

Finally, she told them to let her go, she wasn't going anywhere until the commissioner came, which he did a half hour later. He had brought his detective with him, and they looked at the gruesome scene with distaste. They came to the same conclusion as the gardener, housekeeper, and cook. Marielena was guilty.

Regardless of their conclusions, they asked numerous questions: Where was Charles?; Who else was in the house?; Did they believe that anyone else could have done it?; Where had they been when they heard the scream?; Had they heard any other noises of a struggle or fight?; How long had it taken them to reach the room?; Had Margarita or Marielena eaten breakfast?; Did they know if the portrait sittings had started that morning?; and, Had Marielena confessed? As an off-thought, they asked if they had heard any strange noises anytime during the night? To which all three of the staff and Marielena recounted their own story about the thunderstorms with the brilliant lightning bolts and deafening and rolling thunder which had lasted almost all night. No one had heard anything other than the storm. The gardener thought for a moment and, looking straight at the commissioner, said that he had seen something strange this morning as he walked the grounds looking for damage. He stated, "Near the back gate, almost hidden by a bush, were strange tire tracks."

The commissioner left the detective in the studio with the cook and housekeeper, and he and the gardener walked down and inspected the spot by the gate. Sure enough, there were tire tracks in the mud there. The commissioner thanked the gardener for his observation and sharp eyes. Then the commissioner called for the coroner. The coroner came as the commissioner and detective arrested Marielena. Over her protests that she had arrived only to find Margarita already dead, the detective took her to jail.

Marielena was in shock. Shock that her friend was dead. Shock that she was being blamed for the murder. She couldn't believe that this was happening to her. She couldn't believe that Margarita was dead. She couldn't believe that everyone blamed her. She was dumbfounded. And now she was going to jail for a murder that she hadn't committed.

The commissioner locked Marielena in a cell, and again asked her if she had killed Margarita. When she denied it, he asked the next question which had been in the back of his mind for several weeks, "Are you in love with Charles Elliot?"

With a shocked expression of disbelief on her face, she stated adamantly, "No!"

Then he asked, "Did you kill Margarita so you could have Charles all to yourself?"

Again, she vehemently said, "No!"

But she knew that at this moment in time, he really didn't believe her. All the evidence seemed to point to a love triangle. When the coroner ran the fingerprint test on the handle of the dagger, it only seemed to confirm what everyone thought. Marielena had killed Margarita.

The commissioner called Charles in London at his parent's

manor. He had assured the housekeeper that he, personally, would call Charles when he had gotten the telephone number from her. He told her that it was his unpleasant task to always inform the next of kin when a murder had transpired. Charles needed to know that his beautiful wife was dead. When he reached Charles in London, he explained that Margarita's body had been found in the studio and that all evidence pointed to her killer being the artist, Marielena.

At first Charles had seemed unable to fully understand about the murder; but, at last, he broke down in sobs. As his parents looked aghast at him, they realized that this phone call was a bitterly tragic one and that their son was totally overwhelmed with grief. Charles told them, "I have to return to Spain as soon as I can. Margarita is dead. She was murdered, and I have to see her killer brought to justice."

His mother said, "Oh my dear boy, of course you do," and then, she too broke down and cried.

His father added, "Is there anything that we can do? Do you want us to come with you?"

"No," replied Charles. "I can't imagine how this has happened. I will call you as soon as I have any more information." Smiling to himself as he went upstairs to pack. He could imagine how it had happened - he knew how it had happened. He called for a lift to the London airport. He had a return ticket to Madrid and talked the ticket seller into exchanging it for an immediate flight using his wife's murder as his excuse. Of course, under the circumstances, they were more than happy to oblige him and get him on the next flight.

In Madrid he rented a car to go to the villa. He kept reminding himself that he was the distraught husband and he needed to behave like one. Inwardly, he was so pleased that his plans had gone so well and that all the blame rested on Marielena's shoulders. She was a little nobody whom no one would mourn or even believe. He had chosen his victim well.

In the meanwhile, the coroner consulted with the

commissioner. There were some inconsistences to the theory that Marielena had done the deed. He said that Margarita's body was at room temperature, in fact it was closer to the temperature of the tile floor upon which she lay. If she had so recently screamed and been killed, she would have had a body temperature closer to normal body temperature. Even though he hadn't reached the villa less than an hour after it was presumed that she was killed, there should not be such a discrepancy in body temperature. It didn't make sense. Furthermore, the gardener had found the balcony doors to the room open but the curtains closed. How had the amount of water which was on the floor of the studio come into the room? The curtains and the balcony doors would both have to have been open during the rainstorm during the entire night. Who closed the curtains? And, when? After they discussed the possibilities, the commissioner started to doubt that Marielena had killed Margarita. He told the coroner to put all this information in his report but to keep it a secret from the press, who had now found out that a murder had occurred and was clamoring for information. Margarita had been a celebrity and a rich resident of their village where nothing like this ever happened. Of course, the press would want answers. He thus told the coroner to keep it from everyone, even the murder victim's husband, because he thought that someone was lying. But who? Maybe if all the information was kept secret, the real killer would make a mistake. He decided not to tell any family member, the staff, nor the press. This was one murder which he would solve, but he doubted that he would solve it quickly.

So, when Charles, the supposedly upset and grieving husband, met with the commissioner at the morgue to identify and claim his wife's body, he wanted to know exactly what information the commissioner had concerning the murder and the murderer. The commissioner stated that he was conducting the investigation himself and he would release all information as soon as it was verified. He watched Charles closely to see Charles's reactions.

Chapter 15 - The Discovery

Charles put on a great act by pretending to faint when viewing his wife's lifeless body. As the commissioner grabbed hold of his arm and helped him to a chair, it seemed to Commissioner Rivera that Charles's recovery seemed too quick. His past experience and expertise with grieving relative's reactions gave him a sense that Charles might be faking the extent of his emotions. Oh, yes, Charles asked all the right questions about the discovery of Margarita's body and the presence of Marielena and her prints on the murder weapon. He showed the appropriate anger and indignation and ranted about justice. Then he went into a tirade about having hired the artist to paint a portrait of his wife. He berated himself for inviting her into his home, even to live, while the portrait was being finished. He couldn't believe that he had gone to England leaving Margarita alone in the house with Marielena. He should have seen some hint of hatred between the two women. He postulated that Marielena was jealous of Margarita and was envious of his love for his wife. What had he missed? On and on he went, and Commissioner Rivera was reminded of the Shakespearean line "Me thinks he doth protest too much". The commissioner didn't let on that these thoughts had crossed his mind. At last Charles couldn't stand it any longer and stated loudly, "I told you that she had told me she loved me. I should have known."

Commissioner Rivera responded, "Well, we're still looking at all the facts. Thank you for identifying the body. Now you can make arrangements for her burial or cremation or whatever you plan."

While Charles was not really satisfied with the commissioner's comments, he was too smart to say anything other than, "Thank you."

He went home, canceled the birthday celebration and all its foods, wines, servers, buses, drivers, and everything else. Then he contacted the funeral home to arrange a cremation and funeral. When he spoke to the funeral director, giving him permission to pick up the body at the morgue and to cremate it, he sniffled, blew his nose, and pretended to cry softly. He also contacted Padre Juan to have him deliver the funeral mass and service of burial; and, as he spoke to the priest, he again feigned to break down and sob over the phone. Afterward, he commended himself on his performances. They were genuinely dramatic and had solicited comments from both men of empathy and remorse for his loss. Boy, he was good!

Then, as a good son-in-law, he decided to make airline arrangements and to call Margarita's family in Mallorca. No one had informed them yet of their daughter's demise. When he reached them, he said, "My dear wife, your Margarita, has been murdered. I'm so sorry to tell you, but it was a horrible murder, and I feel responsible. I hired the artist who has been arrested for the crime. I had no idea that she was capable of such a deed." At this he stopped and sobbed over the phone quite convincingly. He continued, "I have arranged for a funeral mass and funeral service; however, there will be no viewing as I am having her cremated. The body was so damaged that a viewing is impossible." At that, he again sobbed loudly. It was a good thing no one was watching him, as there were no tears with the sobs. He went on, "I will arrange transportation for the entire family to be here with her for the mass and service, if that is acceptable? I feel all who loved her should be together to mourn her. I'm even trying to have my parents present; however, my father's health may not allow him to attend. Please help me take care of these last times for and with my beloved wife." He again sobbed for emphasis. When he hung up, he decided that he could receive an award for his acting.

Margarita's parents were dumbstruck. How had this happened to their beautiful daughter? Of course, they would be there for the mass and burial. How could they not? At least they had a son-in-law who was deeply grieving and who had greatly loved their daughter. It was good that he was wealthy enough that they could also be at the mass and service. They made note of the day, and the airline ticket times, and gathered their mourning clothes together. Fortunately, they had a few days yet to make arrangements to miss work so they could travel to the villa.

CHAPTER 16

QUESTIONS

CHAPTER 16

QUESTIONS

Commissioner Rivera decided that he needed to speak to Marielena again. He wasn't at all satisfied that the crime was solved. He made up his mind to call her into his office on the pretext of finding out about whether she had a lawyer or not. He hadn't been contacted by an attorney yet, but it was still early in the case. As she entered his office, he could see how bewildered she was.

He asked her without looking up, "Have you hired a lawyer?"

"No," she responded, "I haven't any money to hire one. My whole life's monies were dependent upon my finishing the portrait and getting the last half of my artist fee. Now I'll never finish, even though it could be considered finished, and I'll never get my payment."

"Then the state will get a lawyer for you."

She looked up expectantly, but said nothing other than, "Oh, I had forgotten about that."

"How do you plan to plead?" He continued.

To which she sobbed and said, "Not guilty. I didn't kill her, I really didn't. We had gotten very close during the painting sessions. She felt like a friend to me. I couldn't have killed her. She had so many problems."

"Problems?" He asked. "She confided in you?" not quite believing what he was hearing.

"Oh, yes," Marielena replied. "We would have long talks as I painted her and between painting sessions too. She trusted me to keep her secrets."

"Can I ask what secrets she told you?" Asked the

commissioner.

Marielena stopped for a while to collect her thoughts. As she started to speak it was as though she were afraid of telling him what Margarita had confided. At last she said, "I guess now she's dead, it won't matter; but I really don't feel that I should betray her confidences. She was so terribly lonely and upset a lot of the time we were together, but especially recently." At that comment, Marielena lapsed into silence.

Commissioner Rivera decided not to say anything. Perhaps, if he didn't prompt her, she would begin speaking again. The silence started becoming uncomfortable for both of them; but he had interviewed so many people over the years and had learned that when the silence continued long enough, most people felt they needed to fill that silence. Sometimes the information which they gave during these times could be very important. So, he waited.

At last, Marielena said, "Not only did she tell me things, but she gave me some things."

The commissioner again waited until Marielena continued, "She suspected Charles of multiple infidelities. She gave me a packet of documents which she thought would prove it."

"Do you know if she discussed this problem with anyone else?"

"Yes, she told me that she'd spoken to Padre Juan during confession and to Pastor Luis at the Protestant church."

"And what had they told her to do?"

"Padre Juan told her to pray. Pastor Luis told her to act like nothing was wrong until she had more information."

"Where did you put this packet?"

"Well- she didn't want it at the villa because Charles might find it, so she had me take it to my attic apartment in the village. She wanted me to hide it."

"And did you?"

"Yes. It's in the bottom and back of my armoire."

"Do I have your permission to get it?"

"Yes. You have my permission. Just ask Señora Santiago to let you into my room."

"And another question before we end for today," the Commissioner paused for a moment for emphasis, "did you ever tell Charles that you were in love with him?"

"Absolutely not," stated Marielena. "He was my employer and Margarita was my friend."

"Didn't he take you home sometimes? And weren't you seen together in the village?"

"Yes, but we only discussed the portrait and the up-coming birthday celebration. The portrait had to be completed on time for the celebration."

At that, the commissioner called his deputy to come and take Marielena back to her cell.

When she had left his office, he got out the coroner's report again. Taking a clean notebook, he started to make a list of things that didn't make sense. Afterward he closed his office door and went into the village to Marielena's room at Señora Santiago's. He found the packet of documents exactly where she had told him it could be found.

He removed the packet and because the hour was late, he took it home with him. He thought he'd take it back to the office in the morning and study it then. He had stopped at the local restaurant on the way home and gotten a carryout dinner. As he opened up the meal, curiosity overcame him. He started going through the packet even while he ate. What he found almost choked him.

Margarita had compiled photos, dates, tabloid articles, and a list of every business meeting which had carried Charles to numerous places where these photos had been taken. Everything documented her husband's infidelities perfectly. The commissioner decided after looking at all the evidence which

Chapter 16 - Questions

Marielena had hidden for Margarita that maybe there were other secrets which Marielena knew about. He finished his now-cold dinner and went to bed. He would proceed with the investigation tomorrow.

The next morning, he took the entire packet with him to work and locked it in his office safe. In the notebook, which he had started keeping the previous day, he continued the following list:

Marielena's fingerprints were on the dagger.

Charles' "confession to him" that Marielena had told him that she loved him.

Marielena's denial of professing love to Charles.

Charles was in England the night of the murder.

Marielena was living in the villa during the murder.

Night of murder were thunderstorms with brilliant thunderbolts and noise.

Margarita's body was colder than it should have been for a recent killing.

Too much water in studio for curtains to be drawn, even though door was open.

Margarita's throat had been slit and she had been stabbed 14 times.

There were too many wounds to have been done between the scream and arrival of staff.

Staff members had arrived on the scene immediately after the murder.

If a struggle had occurred, why had the staff only heard one scream.

Not enough noise for a fight or struggle.

Charles seen in the village with Marielena several times.

Coincidence of hiring an unknown artist new to the village.

Marielena's statement that she knew Margarita had spoken to Padre and Pastor.

Charles seemed to be overwrought at killing, but recovered quickly.

Tire tracks beside gate in garden .

Margarita's packet of evidence showing Charles's infidelities.

There were two items on the list which stood out to him and which he felt he had neglected and now needed to attend to. First, the tire tracks. He must have those tracks preserved. Fortunately, it hadn't rained since the murder. Now was the time to have those tracks filled with plaster of paris and brought into the station before they were destroyed. Second, the assumption that Marielena had told the truth about Margarita speaking with Padre Juan and Pastor Luis. The murder had become common knowledge in the village, but perhaps he was still in time to get some information from Padre Juan and Pastor Luis without that information being too skewed by public opinion.

Since he and Padre Juan were very good friends, he decided to start with him first. He walked over to the Catholic church rectory and knocked on Padre Juan's door. Padre Juan opened the door and invited him into his study. Before he could speak, Padre Juan said, "I've been expecting that you would come here to talk to me."

The commissioner said, "You've heard of Magarita's death of course."

"Yes, her husband called here to arrange her funeral mass and service. Even though he isn't Catholic, he knew she was and had worked here in the church."

"And…?" Commissioner Rivera let his comment trail off as a question.

"And, I have consented to it. She was a wonderful woman and worked very hard with our young church members. Tragic!"

"It seems she and her husband had some problems?"

"Yes, she couldn't have children which she wanted badly."

"And her husband?"

"She told me that he was looking into finding an adoption agency that was suitable so they could adopt a child or children."

"Was that the only problem which she told you about?"

Chapter 16 - Questions

The Padre's face registered some surprise, but he quickly regained his composure. He was silent for a moment and then said, "No, but the rest of what she told me was in her Confession. I can't divulge that, of course."

Determining that he would get no further with the priest, Commissioner Rivera left the rectory berating himself. He should have known that anything Margarita had told the priest in Confession wouldn't be repeated to him. He hoped, however, under the circumstances the Padre might tell him. But no. Evidently his vows of silence were too strong, even in the case of murder.

As Commissioner Rivera walked to the small Protestant church, he hoped strongly that Pastor Luis would be more forthcoming. And he was. Pastor Luis, after commenting on the tragedy of Margarita's death, sat quietly for a few minutes before he asked, "Did her husband kill her for what she knew?"

Commissioner Rivera thought. Ah! Now we get to it.

He asked the Pastor to divulge his conversation with Margarita. And, slowly, the Pastor filled in all her comments to him concerning her distrust of her husband and how, with a description of the lengthy compilation of photos, dates, tabloid articles, and business trips' dates, she had shown him her evidence. Commissioner Rivera wrote down more notes in his notebook. He then told the Pastor that what he had just revealed to him and what he had discussed with Margarita should not be told to anyone else. "The town's people are already abuzz, talking about the murder. We don't need to give them more to discuss. After all, these bits of information are part of my search for truth in the murder investigation." He finished, "The time will come later for telling what you know. I thank you for your honesty today. This information will be added to what I have already discovered."

MORE QUESTIONS

CHAPTER 17

MORE QUESTIONS

Commissioner Rivera went to the widow Santiago's again, not to get anything from her, but to talk to her about her impressions of Marielena. After all, she was her landlady; and, she might have a different perspective of her and her life.

He knocked on the door and, as the señora opened it, he said, "I'm sorry to disturb you again, but I really need some information about your renter, Marielena."

She quietly invited him in and said, "What do you want to know?"

"What kind of person is Marielena?"

"I'm not sure I know what you mean?" She replied.

"Oh, let me rephrase that. What was your first impression of her when she asked to rent a room from you?"

"She seemed like a nice young lady- down on her luck. Willing to work hard to advance." She paused for a moment and then added, "Trustworthy- I wouldn't have allowed her in my house if I hadn't thought that."

"Was she always prompt paying her rent?"

"Oh yes. In fact, when she got the down payment from Señor Elliot, she paid all her rent in advance." She paused and then continued, "I think before that she paid her rent even before she ate. I think she sometimes went without food so that she could pay me."

"Did she ever ask for an extension so she could pay you later?"

"Oh, no!" Señora Santiago stated, "She seemed to be a reliable person."

Chapter 17 - More Questions

"Did she ever have anyone up to her room?"

"No. She didn't know many people in the village. She had just moved here from Rhonda."

"Even Señor Elliot?"

"Oh that- the couple of times he dropped her off, she came into the house very quickly. And the two times he just dropped by, she seemed embarrassed and met him outside, like she was surprised to see him and didn't want him here."

"She never invited him inside?"

"No, she didn't. I suppose I'm sort of a busybody, always looking out the windows at my neighbors and what's happening in the neighborhood; but she really seemed to be aware that her actions would always be judged. She tried to live an upstanding life. I just can't imagine her killing Margarita Elliot."

"So, you like Marielena?"

"Very much. Is that all you wanted to know?"

"Yes. I think so for now. If I think of anything else, I'll have to bother you later."

"No problem. I'll be here. Could you please tell her hello for me?"

"Of course. If you'd like to visit her at the jail, I think she might like that. She has had no visitors and probably feels all alone and it seems that no one cares."

"Oh, the poor dear. Of course, I'll come down, but I've never visited anyone at the jail before. I'm not sure I would know how."

"Don't worry. Just ask for myself or my deputy and we'll show you in." He told her goodbye and left, thinking to himself that Marielena at least had one person, beside the Padre, who thought her an upstanding citizen.

He needed to talk to Marielena again. He retraced his steps, he went to his office, and asked that she be brought in again. So far, no lawyer had been assigned to counsel her, and she didn't seem to realize that she shouldn't speak to him without counsel present. He decided to take advantage of that fact before the situation changed.

As she settled down in the seat opposite him, he asked, "Were there any other strange things that happened during the days you were at the villa- even from the very beginning? Were there any other secrets that Margarita told you?"

She thought for a moment and then said, "Yes, I've been thinking about the whole thing, and everything I saw or heard during the entire time. I haven't anything else to do while I've been here and there's a lot that doesn't make sense to me."

"Such as?" He prompted.

"Well, for one thing, I'm not sure why I was hired to paint Margarita. I'm new here. I don't have a reputation in this area of Spain that someone as wealthy as the Elliots would hire me. Why me? At first, I was flattered, but I've been thinking that there was a reason for me to be in the house when she was killed."

"Anything else?"

"Yes, the dagger that she was killed with. Charles told me that it had belonged to Margarita's grandfather; but when I asked her about it, she denied it. She stated that such an expensive dagger could never have been in her poor family. She said that she had never seen it before Charles had decided to use it as a symbolic item in her portrait background. Even though Charles had selected all the items, he acted like he didn't know enough about still life paintings to arrange everything on the table. No wonder my fingerprints were on the dagger. He had me arrange all the items, including the dagger."

"And the bedroom where they put me was as far away from the portrait studio room as possible. If anything happened there, I couldn't have seen or heard anything from where I was."

"Oh," said Commissioner Rivera. "What about the studio - anything about that room?"

"Yes." She added, "It wasn't arranged correctly. There

weren't enough lights, so Charles had to get more. And I needed tarpaulins for the floor to protect the tiles, so I had to go the garage and get a large one. Oh!" She stopped for a moment. "What did you and the gardener find when you left the other day? Did I overhear you say there were some sort of tracks in the garden?"

"Yes, near the back gate. They were too small for a car. Maybe a bicycle."

She thought for a moment and then asked, "Did you find a bicycle anywhere on the property? Because there was one in the garage underneath some tarpaulins when I went there to get one for the studio."

"In the garage?"

"Yes."

"What kind of bicycle?"

"It was an old-fashioned one, rusted and scraped. The kind my older brother had. Not the fancy racing bikes you see now that the youngsters ride with gears. It had patches of red paint on it, as though it had been all red at one time but was old and most of the original paint was gone."

"Did it have fat tires too?"

"Yes. Not the narrow ones you see now."

Commissioner Rivera took out his notebook and added some arrows to the list with notes beside some items. He then turned a couple of pages, put down some more questions scribbling furiously. In one area he wrote - look for a bicycle. He thought for a moment and then said, "Why did you hide Margarita's evidence against her husband?"

"Because we had become friends and I knew she trusted me."

"Anything else?"

"Yes, I've been wondering if Charles ever ordered a frame for the portrait. I asked him if he was going to frame it, and he told me that he would frame it in gold. It's such a huge canvas that I had to order it special. The frame would also have to have been ordered special and the celebration of Margarita's birthday would have been this week - right? So, he would have had to have placed an order for the frame. Right?"

"And the portrait was to be hung for the celebration?"

"Yes."

"Where would he have ordered the frame?"

"Maybe one of the large companies in Madrid."

'Are you thinking that maybe he knew there wouldn't be a celebration? Maybe he knew she'd be dead and the frame wouldn't be needed?"

"It would make sense."

Commissioner Rivera made another note in his notebook.

"Only one more thing, "she added. "It was very convenient that he was in England when she was murdered - and that it occurred during a huge thunderstorm when it would be very noisy to cover the murder noises."

Commissioner Rivera thought to himself, how did he do it? Or did he?

After he had released her to go back to her cell, cautioning her to keep quiet about his questions, he went to the villa. He said he needed to double check a couple of things. He retracted his steps to the back gate. As he thought, the bicycle tracks still remained in the earth. He went to the garage and checked out the tarpaulins where Marielena had seen them. There was no bicycle there, but there were a pair of glasses and a rubber glove that looked like they had been dropped near the garbage can. Whose glasses and whose rubber glove?

He went back to his car and retrieved an evidence bag and department issued rubber gloves. He collected the two items, deciding that he needed to send them to the forensic lab to check for fingerprints and DNA. He called the detective to come and meet him at the villa and to bring plaster of paris and a big plastic evidence box. Even though a few days had lapsed since he had decided to do this, it still hadn't rained and now it was imperative that they collect these tracks. The detective came immediately and together they preserved the tire tracks. Afterward the detective took them back to the police station.

Commissioner Rivera reentered the villa and asked the housekeeper if Charles had cancelled all the purchases for the birthday celebration. Paula showed him the list of orders and their check-offs beside them indicating that they had been cancelled. Under the pretext of worrying about Charles and his mental condition of grieving, he asked, "Do you know if he cancelled his order for the frame for the portrait?"

She answered him, "No. I don't think he'd ordered one yet."

"Wasn't the portrait to have been unveiled at the birthday celebration?"

"Yes," she said thoughtfully. "That would have been this week. Obviously, he must have ordered a frame for the portrait. But - I was not made aware of the order. Usually, when anything is ordered, I see the invoice, and am made aware of the arrival date of the delivery. And I wasn't made aware of any invoice nor any delivery date. Have you spoken to Charles about it?"

"Not yet. He must have simply forgotten about it."

"That's not like him. He has almost a photographic memory for things like that."

Then Commissioner Rivera asked, "What company delivered the canvas and easel?"

"When Marielena ordered them and they were delivered, the same morning that she started work on the portrait, the truck had a sign on it called 'Artístico Mejor'. I remember vividly as I told them where to park in order to make the delivery into the villa."

He made note of the name in his notebook.

The next day he had his deputy call 'Artistíco Mejor' and every frame and art store within 200 kilometers of the village. Surely, Charles wouldn't order a frame from further away than that. There had been no sales nor order of frame of the appropriate size within the last year. There also were no pending orders waiting to be filled. Charles hadn't ordered a frame for the portrait. Extremely interesting.

CHAPTER 18

THE COVERED TRAIL

CHAPTER 18
THE COVERED TRAIL

Commissioner Rivera sat in his office and thought hard. He went over everything that he already knew up to that day about the case. Somehow Charles had either killed his wife himself, or maybe he had someone else kill her. Although Charles seemed to have a foolproof alibi and all the circumstantial evidence pointed to Marielena, that evidence had been planted by Charles himself from what he could understand. The facts that he had recorded in his notebook just didn't add up. He needed to start at the beginning and review everything that he could prove.

He started by walking from his office to the back alleyway behind the villa. He had always approached the villa coming up to the front of the villa from the main road. If a bicycle were the means of transport for the killer and the tracks were found near the back gate, then the path the killer must have taken would have been through that back gate and the connecting alleyway. On the way up to the villa, he looked at the terrain, the condition of the alleyway, and the surrounding buildings. Reaching the villa, he started at the gate and walked slowly downhill toward the village. This would have been the exit from the villa which the killer would have traveled. What if he were on a bicycle? Where would he go? What would be his destination to get away from the murder scene?

He continued down the hill. So far, the condition of the alleyway would have been rough, but passable for anyone on a bike. It would have been dark and wet; but, if the person were careful, the cobbles were smooth enough that it would have been possible to go quickly, especially downhill. The alleyway followed downhill and joined a street where the road conditions were even better. This street then crossed the river at a bridge where he stopped and looked down. The flood waters had receded from the heavy rains; and there, directly under the bridge, was the partially buried remains of a bicycle.

Leaving the road above, he went down under the bridge and dragged the bicycle out of the surrounding debris. It was an old bicycle, rusted and scraped, with patches of red paint. And the tires were broad, not narrow. He called his detective and they took the bicycle back to the station where they matched its tires with the plaster of paris mold they had made of the tire tracks behind the villa. They matched perfectly. So - the possible murderer could have ridden the bicycle to the village and thrown it into the river to get rid of evidence. Had the murderer thrown anything else into the river from the bridge? Would it have floated downstream? He and his detective went back to the river to look. It would be almost too much good luck if they found anything. The waters had been deep and running swiftly the night of the murder and most of the next day. They searched the river and the banks almost three kilometers downstream. They found nothing. If the killer had thrown anything else away that night, it was gone.

Commissioner Rivera returned to his office to think. He tried to estimate the window of time when Margarita had to have been killed. If the killer had planned well, the murder had occurred during the thunderstorm with everyone in bed. With all the noises of the storm, no one had heard anything. They all had to have been in bed so that they wouldn't disrupt the murder. The hour would have had to be very late or very early - perhaps in the wee hours of the morning so that no one would be up yet. And, it had to have been still dark enough that no one would be on the streets. The killer wouldn't want to be seen nor recognized. Again, he tried to put himself in the killer's mind. What would the killer have done when he reached the village? The killer had thrown away his means of transportation at the river. Now he would have been on foot. The killer needed a way out of town. Either someone was meeting him or he was going to have to rent a taxi, take a bus or train, or have a car stashed somewhere. Commissioner Rivera then considered the time of day that this would have occurred. There was no way that he could be able to follow the trail if the killer had someone waiting for him somewhere, but what if he had done this all alone without help? Commissioner River next went to the taxi company and asked if they had a record of anyone hiring a taxi at that early morning hour on the day of question. No, no record. He then went to the car rental company, there was only one in town. Again, no record of anyone renting a car nor picking one up at that time of day on the murder date. He thought that maybe the car had been rented in Toledo the night before, driven to the village, and returned the next day. None of the car rental companies in Toledo had any matching records for the involved days or times. Dead end.

Commissioner Rivera thought - no car nor taxi involved. He consulted the bus schedules. There hadn't been any buses at that time of day. The bus schedule didn't start until after dawn. By that time the killer would have wanted to be long gone and to remain unseen on the village streets. Next, he went to the train station in the village, but again there weren't any trains at that hour. But what if the killer hadn't taken a train from the village, what if he had walked to Toledo and taken a train there? He could remain completely unseen in the village that way, especially if it were still dark. It really wasn't that far to walk from the village to Toledo if one were in good physical shape. He, himself, had done it many times. It was strenuous, but really didn't take that much time. And, if it were early enough in the morning, the killer might be able to take the earliest train from Toledo and remain unseen in the process. He consulted the train schedules in Toledo. Sure enough, the first train from Toledo to Madrid left exactly when he had guessed. The time that someone would have had to take that train was perfect, if they had murdered Margarita, rode a bicycle down the hill to the village, thrown the bicycle (and whatever) into the river, walked quickly into Toledo, and made that first train to Madrid. Ah - but had someone seen the killer? That was the next question.

Chapter 18 - The Covered Trail

The next morning, he went to the train station in Toledo before that first train left for Madrid. He knew it was a long shot, but he had to try. Looking at the people standing there waiting for that train, he asked if they were commuters and if they regularly took this first train to Madrid. He wrote down their names and contact information. Then he asked them if they remembered anyone getting on this train with them that usually didn't ride with them. Several of the group thought for awhile and two of them stated that, "Yes, about a week ago, the morning after the horrible rain storm which we all talked about when we were waiting for this train, there was a man who got on the train with us who had never ridden it before."

"Someone new to your group of early commuters?"

"I had never seen him before," stated one of the two.

"Can you describe him?" Asked Commissioner Rivera.

"He was dressed all in dark colors and had a huge backpack. He kept to himself and sat alone."

The other commuter added, "He was blond with a goatee."

"Did he have glasses? Or any other distinguishing features?"

"No, he didn't have any glasses."

Commissioner Rivera then asked again, "You're sure that you had never seen him before?"

"No, he was a complete stranger."

"Where do you all go when you reach Toledo?"

"To work," they all responded.

"And the morning in question?"

One of the two who had volunteered information stated, "I think that this man went directly from the train into the men's room. I saw him enter there as I walked past."

"Did any of you also enter the restroom?"

They all answered, "No."

Commissioner Rivera joined the commuters as they

boarded the train for Madrid. The question as to where the murderer went at the train station in Madrid needed to be answered. At least now he had some sort of a description to follow.

When he reached the Madrid train station, he went to the main offices, introduced himself to the station manager, told him that he was tracing a lead in a murder investigation, and asked to see the security camera footage of the station on the morning in question. Since it was a matter of police business, he was allowed to go through the security cameras' footages. Their security system made the job easier because the dates and times were on the videos.

As he watched the videos of the morning in question, he found one with the commuters on it and the man whom they had described. He did go into the men's room carrying his backpack, but he didn't come out. Who came out, because the backpack was recognizable in later footage, was a man who had black hair, glasses, and a mustache, as well as different clothes. He was also carrying a plastic bag, rather full, in his hand. He proceeded through the terminal. His progress could be traced from one security camera's video to another.

As he walked through the terminal, he stopped at each trash container and left some sort of item from his bag in each. At the last trash container, he deposited the now empty trash bag. Then he went to a kiosk and purchased another train ticket. Following on the security camera videos, he was seen to quickly walk to a different train platform where a train was preparing to leave for Paris. The train personnel in the office confirmed the destination and time that the man's train left. Commissioner Rivera signed for all the videos as evidence which would be used by him in his police investigation. He was happy that he had followed his instincts and gone to Madrid that morning. Returning to Toledo and then to the village and the police station, he went to his office and put the videos into his safe with his other items of the investigation. It had been a productive day.

Chapter 18 - The Covered Trail

His detective came in and informed him that Marielena had finally been assigned a lawyer who was speaking to her in an interrogation room. Commissioner Rivera had wanted to speak with her before he left for the day, but decided it was better if he didn't. He really didn't want to give her any false hope. He decided that he would follow his lead from Madrid to Paris the next day, went home, packed a small overnighter, and slept soundly.

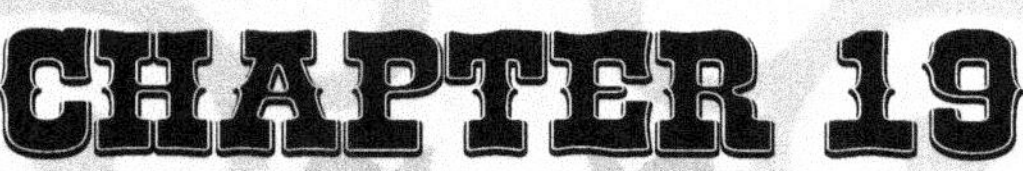

CHAPTER 19

FOLLOWING THE COVERED TRAIL

CHAPTER 19
FOLLOWING THE COVERED TRAIL

Commissioner Rivera called the office as soon as he knew his deputy would be there that morning. He said, "You know I followed a possible lead yesterday, but you weren't in the office when I got there last night. I need to tell you about it."

Deputy Orlando responded, "Yes, how did that go?"

"It was very interesting. A possible suspect took a train from Toledo to Madrid; but in Madrid he took another train to Paris. I'm sure it was the same man even though he was in a different disguise because he carried the same backpack and wore the same shoes."

"Are we going to trace him further? You said he took a train to Paris?"

"Yes. Yesterday when I went to Toledo, some witnesses gave me a good description of a man who boarded a train from Toledo at a time which matched a possible murderer leaving Toledo for Madrid. Since I had a good description, I took the train to Madrid. I had no trouble getting videos of that man from the security cameras in the Madrid train station. The videos then lead me to a second description of the same man who boarded a train to Paris. I've packed my overnighter and today, I'll try to find traces of him in Paris. I'm leaving you in charge of the office while I'm gone - probably two or three days."

"OK. Is there anything else that you want me to take care of?" Asked Deputy Orlando.

"Keep an eye on Marielena while I'm gone. I've locked all the evidence which we've collected so far on the case in the office safe. Don't tell anyone, but I think this is a very productive lead which I've found. We may solve this murder sooner than I anticipated."

Commissioner Rivera then took an early train to Madrid and another to Paris. He arrived by early afternoon. Armed with the suspect's description, he went to the train office and again, after much red tape and identifying himself as a policeman following a murder suspect, he was allowed to view the video footages of the station's security cameras. Since he knew the exact time of arrival of the train which had come from Madrid, he had no trouble finding the suspect again on the security tapes. He watched the suspect go through the same procedure through the station in Paris as he had in Madrid. However, when the suspect left the men's room here, the suspect had medium brown hair and a beard. The same backpack was being carried and he wore the same shoes. Then the suspect purchased a ticket for London and boarded that train. Now Commissioner Rivera knew he had to go to London. Unfortunately. There was only a late train which he could take. He purchased a ticket and left for London late that evening. So late in fact, that by the time he arrived, the station offices were closed. The ticket counters and kiosks were open, but he needed to speak with the station manager. He made note of the time that the station office opened in the morning, left the station, and went to the nearest hotel. He checked in, went to a nearby restaurant for dinner, and then went back to the hotel for the night.

The next morning, after an early wakeup call and breakfast, he arrived back at the train station. It turned out he had to navigate the same red tape with the station manager as he had experienced at the Paris station; but, after looking at the videos from the security cameras, the results were even better. He saw the suspect with medium brown hair and a beard arriving on the train from Paris and entering the London men's water closet; but the suspect who walked out, carrying the same backpack and wearing the same shoes, was Charles Elliot. Bingo!

Commissioner Rivera obtained the video footages as evidence and left the train station. Then, knowing that Charles was presently in Spain, decided that, while he was in England, he should go to see Charles's parents. He would inquire about their feelings about their deceased daughter-in-law, would inquire about their memories of Margarita and Charles's marriage, and would extend his condolences to them about their "loss". Maybe, he might find out something that could further his case against his suspect, their son Charles.

He rented a car and drove to their mansion. When he rang the doorbell, a maid opened it and inquired as to who he was and what was his business. He explained and said he needed to speak to the Elliots about Margarita, Charles's now deceased wife. Lady Anne greeted him cordially, explaining that her husband was sleeping and that Charles wasn't at home.

Commissioner Rivera extended his condolences to her. He stated, "While I really didn't know your daughter-in-law well, her death has been a great loss to our community."

Lady Anne replied, "We have been devastated by her death and will do anything we can to see that the murderer is brought to justice. My husband is an invalid, but I, personally will do my best in speaking for both of us."

The commissioner was quiet for a moment and then he said, "I understand that Charles was here in England on a business trip the night of Margarita's murder."

"Yes. The night that Margarita, poor dear, was murdered in Spain, he told us not to disrupt him as he was going to take a sedative, go to bed early, and try to "sleep off" whatever was making him feel ill. He thought that he might have picked up some kind of a 'bug'".

"Would you have noticed anything unusual that evening after Charles retired for the night?"

Lady Anne thought for moment and remembered the strange person she had seen in the yard that evening. She remembered that the person was the same size as her son but hadn't looked like him. She had sent the gardener out to look for that person. She had been silent for several moments thinking.

Chapter 19 - Following the Covered Trail

That person couldn't have been her son. But what if it had been? Could Charles be so deceitful? Her answer to herself was, yes. She thought about his infidelities - at least the ones she knew of. What if?

Commissioner Rivera had sat quietly waiting for her reply. He had considered breaking the silence, but, as usual, decided the quiet would work as well for him as further questions. At last he said, "Lady Anne?"

She seemed to come back to herself and answered, "Yes. There was something strange that evening. My husband and I were seated in the dining room eating dinner. I got up to close the shutters. As I looked out the window, I saw a man about the size of my son in the yard; but I decided that it had to be a stranger who had gotten into the yard. I sent the gardener out to investigate. By the time he reached the back yard, there was no one there."

"Can you describe the man?"

"Well - he had on some kind of glasses and long grey hair, almost down to his shoulders. He was dressed all in black, but it could have been another dark color. It was getting dark and he seemed to be almost running in the yard. He stayed in the shadows so it was hard to see."

"Had you ever seen him before?"

"No."

"Which way was he moving?"

"He was moving toward the garage."

"Was he carrying anything?"

"No. As I mentioned earlier, it was starting to get dark, but I saw him clearly enough to see that he wasn't carrying anything."

"Did anyone else see him?"

"No. My husband was in his wheelchair and he wouldn't have been able to see out the windows."

Commissioner Rivera thought for a few moments and then asked, "Did you hear any sounds from Charles's room during the night?"

"No, but I really didn't listen too hard. I assumed that he was doing what he said he was, taking a sedative and sleeping."

"What was Charles like in the morning when he woke up?"

"He seemed to feel better. He said he was glad he'd taken the medicine. He ate breakfast."

"What time was that?"

"Just after noon," she replied.

"In other words, he had a very long night to sleep?"

"Yes," she answered.

Commissioner Rivera decided to change the subject. "If you don't mind, I'd like to ask you about Charles and Margarita's marriage. Do you know if they were having any problems?"

"Yes,' she said. "They wanted to have children, but Margarita couldn't have children - some physical problem. They were going to adopt, but, somehow, they never got around to it. We were upset, but eventually realized that their adopting a child would give the family an heir."

"Do you know if Charles was faithful in his marriage?"

She looked up at him quickly and answered, "I don't think he was. I think there was someone else he was interested in. He never told me, but there were rumors. I checked up on some information which a close friend had told me." She didn't say anymore.

"May I see his room? If not, I can obtain a search warrant and come back later."

"You really suspect him then?"

"Unfortunately, yes."

"Oh dear."

She stood up after a few minutes and continued, "Charles has not always been the son that I thought he was or that maybe he wanted me to believe that he was. Maybe we'd better go to his room and look around."

CHAPTER 20

CHARLES' ROOM

CHAPTER 20

CHARLES' ROOM

Commissioner Rivera stood and followed Lady Anne up the stairs to her son's room. After looking around, he went to the window and opened it. It opened so easily that he was surprised until he saw the layer of grease that had been placed in the frame opening. He poked his head out of the window and looked down and around at the yard. Then he called Lady Anne to the window. He pointed to the grease and told her that the window opened more easily than he had anticipated. Then he pointed to the heavy vines, like a stepladder leading to the ground. They noticed that some of the branches had been broken off.

She sat down with a heavy sigh of resignation. It was as if she could see her son both entering and leaving his room by this window and the natural ladder outside. Then she jumped up and again looked out the window. Her eyes moved from under Charles's window to the garage. She thought about that path. It was the same path the strange man had taken the night of Margarita's murder.

Commissioner Rivera watched her. He knew that she was thinking the same thing that he was. At last she said, "It had to have been my son." Commissioner Rivera assumed she meant, not only the man in the yard that she had seen had been her son, but the murderer also had to have been her son. He asked her, "Do I have your permission to examine his entire room, its adjoining bath, and its closet?"

"Yes, in fact I'll help you," she answered.

Together they searched everything. All drawers were turned out, all clothes were gone through, and even under the bed was examined. Everything in the closet was laid out on the bed. And, finally, in the back of the closet they found the huge backpack with its contents.

Commissioner Rivera and Lady Anne looked at all the contents. One of the passports had a picture of a blond man with a goatee, one had a picture of a medium brown-haired man with a beard, another had a picture of a black-ha red man with horned rimmed glasses and a mustache, and the last one was a gray long-haired man with plastic-framed glasses. He passed that passport to Lady Anne. She quickly said, "That's the man that I saw," and started to cry.

As Commissioner Rivera went through all the papers, clothes, business cards, and credit cards from the backpack, he thought of another thing. "Have you ever seen this backpack before?" he asked her.

"No, I haven't." She said.

"Does Charles have anywhere else he stays when he comes to London?"

"Yes, he has his own apartment in London where he sometimes stays. Or he is at the company business." Lady Anne said.

"Would it be possible to see those two places?" he asked.

"Yes," she answered. "I'll take you there myself."

"May I take the backpack and its contents with me?" he asked.

She answered, "Of course. You'll need all that to prove my son's guilt."

She left him for about twenty minutes. She checked on her husband, dressed to go out, and carrying her purse and coat she rejoined him. Before they got into his rental car, he put the backpack in the boot of the car. Together they drove into London and went to Charles's apartment. After an inspection there in which they found several items of women's clothing which were not appropriately sized for Margarita, they continued to the business offices. Again, Commissioner Rivera asked to view security tapes of the offices during the week of Margarita's death. The week when Charles had been in London on business. The tapes of the main entrance showed nothing, but the tape of the garage area showed Charles carrying a briefcase and the large backpack.

Lady Anne said, "Well that about does it, doesn't it?"

Commissioner Rivera stated, "Yes, and I'll have to take this video of the garage with me too." Lady Anne signed all the forms for the security video to be given to him. Then he drove Lady Anne back to the mansion. He asked her if she wanted him to come in to speak with her husband. He also asked her if she and her husband would be coming to Spain for Margarita's funeral mass and funeral.

"My husband won't, but I'll be there," she answered.

"And, would you like me to speak with Lord Edward?" he asked again.

"No," she said, "this is something which I need to do by myself. It might look like the two of us were ganging up on him with this horrible news. I don't think his health would stand up to that. I think I can do it more gently alone. I promise we will not contact Charles. If he thinks he's succeeded in pulling this off and no one suspects anything; let him. He has always done everything he wanted. I'm sure there have been other things that we never knew about nor even suspected. Maybe it's time that all the truth comes out. In the meantime, you do what you need to do and I'll do what I need to do."

As Charles mother entered the mansion, even knowing that Lord Edward was waiting for her in his wheelchair in the drawing room, she went up to her bedroom. She changed into a dress which she knew her husband particularly liked on her and then came back downstairs. As she entered the drawing room she pulled her husband's wheelchair near her, sat down opposite him with her hands holding his, and said, "I bring some sad news."

"Oh, my dear, what?" He asked.

Chapter 20 - Charles' Room

"The gentleman who was here and to whom I've been speaking, went out with, and just returned, is a police commissioner from Spain. I'm sorry you were sleeping when he arrived, and I didn't want to bother you, but now I must."

"Is he investigating our dear Margarita's murder?"

"Yes, Edward."

"And did the artist murder her? Or someone else?"

"Yes, he knows who murdered her. And I may have to go to Spain, probably after Margarita's funeral, to testify at a trial."

"Who did such a thing?"

"My dear," she said quietly, "I have no good way to tell you." She paused. Then she reminded him of the strange man in the yard the night that Margarita had been murdered. He vaguely remembered the incident. She finished by saying, "The stranger in our yard was our son in disguise."

"Why would he want to be in a disguise?"

"Think about what he could have been up to."

Lord Edward was silent for a moment and then said, "Oh, my stars. Not our Charles?"

"Yes, my dear. There is proof that he left England that night, went to Spain, killed his wife, and returned the next morning."

"Have you seen the proof?"

"Not all of it, but enough to believe that he was the murderer."

Lord Edward slumped in his wheelchair. After a few seconds he reached into his pocket for a handkerchief and cried into it softly.

CHAPTER 21

FUNERAL, RELEASE, AND ARREST

CHAPTER 21

FUNERAL, RELEASE, AND ARREST

Commissioner Rivera returned to Spain with all the documentation and the backpack. He thought he had almost everything he needed. When he reached his office, he called for a joint meeting with Deputy Orlando, the coroner, his detective, and the district attorney. He asked if the DNA results had been completed on the glove and the glasses which had been found in the villa's garage. His detective reported that while the DNA on the glove was inconclusive, the DNA on the glasses matched Charles's DNA. They had obtained Charles's DNA from some of his clothing and other possessions taken from the villa. Then the commissioner went over all the evidence which he had accumulated: the eyewitness accounts from the Toledo train station, the video tapes, the plaster of paris mold of tire tracks from the garden, the bicycle, the schedules of the trains which the suspect had taken, the backpack, and all the items from that backpack. He stated that Charles's mother was willing to testify at the trial even though it was against her own son. There were two things missing - the purchase of the bicycle and the non-purchase of a picture frame for Margarita's portrait. With the telephone log of his deputy calling every frame and art store within 200 kilometers and the housekeeper's statement, that if there had been an invoice and order for a frame, she would have known about it, he seemed confident that there had been no frame ordered. He concluded that it would be really beneficial to the coming trial if they could find where the bicycle came from and who had purchased it. They discussed each item carefully and vowed that all the information of their discussion should remain "in house only". Commissioner Rivera then adjourned the meeting.

Chapter 21 - Funeral, Release, and Arrest

Commissioner Rivera copied the passport photos and then started looking in second-hand and bicycle shops in the same 200 kilometer area which they had searched for a source for a picture frame. He found a second-hand store in Madrid where the owner admitted selling an old bicycle which matched the description of the one which had been found in the river. Commissioner Rivera went to the shop and asked the owner if he remembered the purchaser of the bike. The owner stated, "I don't get much business selling old bicycles anymore. All the young people seem to want the racing-kind of bicycles so I was happy when a man came in asking about the old bike which he had seen in the window. Yes, I could probably remember him, especially if I saw him again."

Commissioner Rivera showed him the copied photos from the passports. The owner quickly pointed to the photo of the black-haired man having a mustache and wearing horned-rimmed glasses. What was even more amazing to Commissioner Rivera, the horned-rimmed glasses matched the glasses that he had found in the garage the week of the murder. Commissioner Rivera then showed the owner a photo of the bicycle that had been taken from the river and asked, "Is this the bicycle which the man purchased?"

The owner said, "Yes, that's the bicycle. I should have a copy of the sales receipt here somewhere. Let me look as I have all sales recorded by date." Several minutes later he returned with a copy of the receipt. Unfortunately, the receipt was a cash sale, not credit so there was no signature to be compared. It really didn't matter at that point as the photos of both the buyer and the bicycle had been identified. Plus, as a bonus, the glasses which were on the buyer's face and which were now in the police evidence file, had DNA on them matching Charles Elliot. Commissioner Rivera ended the day at the police station checking in the rest of his evidence collected that day and making more notes in his notebook.

The next morning was the funeral mass and funeral

for Margarita. Even though few people in the village knew her personally, the small church was filled to overflowing. After all, she was a celebrity and Spaniards love the royals and celebrities.

Charles had arranged for his mother and Margarita's large family to occupy the front rows. Everyone was in black and it was a very somber congregation which gathered together. The small urn with her ashes sat on a small, draped table in front of the altar. The townspeople whispered back and forth to each other and gawked at the family and Charles. As the mass began Charles wished that he were anywhere other than sitting in the church. He was exceeding glad he wasn't religious, wasn't Catholic, and didn't believe in anything other than himself. He was above this mass of grievers, onlookers, and religious fanatics. He hoped he was maintaining his poker face and looked sufficiently morose. After all, he was the aggrieved.

Margarita's parents recited the mass responses, held their rosaries, and periodically wiped the tears which ran down their faces. Charles had to remind himself to show signs of grief, and even though there were no tears on his face, he wiped his face anyway. The mass seemed to have no ending, but when it did conclude, the entire congregation followed the priest and the urn to the adjoining village cemetery where Charles had purchased a plot and had erected a large gravestone with angels on top. He thought it added a nice touch. He was so glad to be rid of Margarita that any tombstone would have been fine with him, but he was playing a part and he intended to cover all the bases of being the devastated husband.

All the family went back with him to the villa when the funeral was over. Paula and Isa had arranged a post funeral dinner for the immediate family. That night every guest bedroom in the villa was occupied because Margarita's entire family and Charles's mother stayed with him. The next morning Margarita's family left for Mallorca, but Charles's mother, pretending to want to stay and comfort Charles, stated that she would be staying for at least another week. He couldn't refuse her and still stick to his charade.

Chapter 21 - Funeral, Release, and Arrest

The following morning Commissioner Rivera met with Marielena's lawyer. He called Deputy Orlando into the office as well to be a witness to what he was going to do. When they were settled into the office chairs, Commissioner Rivera told the lawyer that he was going to release Marielena and he wanted them to be present when he told her the good news. The deputy went back into the jail and brought Marielena back to the office. When she entered, he told her to take the only empty chair in the room. She looked at everyone there and said, "Why have you brought me here? Is there going to be a trial today? Or, if not today, when will it be?"

Her lawyer said, "Yes, there will be a trial, but you will not be the accused."

Commissioner Rivera then said, "Marielena, you are no longer a suspect in the murder of Margarita. All the information which you gave me or told me about Margarita and her husband has been checked and rechecked. Everything was true. You are released. You are a free woman."

Marielena could scarcely believe it and said, "Really?"

"Really. But I must ask you not to say anything to anyone about what I've just said. We want you to go home. Don't go out into the village. Don't answer your door. Leave everything to me."

With tears in her eyes, she looked at the commissioner and said, "Thank you."

Marielena did as he had instructed her, but she had to stop at the market to get a few groceries where she ran into Isa, the Elliot's cook. The cook looked surprised to see her, but said nothing other than, "Hello". Marielena was happy that she hadn't needed to talk to Isa and quickly left for her attic room.

Isa, however, also went home quickly and shared the news with Paula, the housekeeper, that she had seen Marielena at the supermarket. Paula and she were discussing Marielena in the kitchen when Charles enter the kitchen to ask when he could expect dinner to be served that evening. He had to inform his mother what time to be ready to dine. The two women looked up quickly at his voice and stopped speaking. He asked, "What did I just overhead about Marielena?"

Isa answered, "She was in the supermarket this afternoon."

"That can't be," he said, "she's in jail."

Isa answered, "Well, she may have been in jail, but she isn't there now."

"Where is she?"

"I don't know."

Charles went into the hall, put on his coat, and drove down to the police station. It was after 8:00 PM and many people were hurrying to get home to dinner as he arrived. He strode into the office and asked to see the commissioner.

He was ushered into the commissioner's office by Deputy Orlando who didn't leave but stood quietly by the door. The commissioner was working on some papers on his desk and looked up as Charles entered, saying, "Oh, Mr. Elliot, how are you?"

"Angry. I understand that the artist, Marielena has been released from jail."

"That is correct, "said the commissioner.

"Can you tell me why?" Said Charles indignantly. "You have all the proof."

"Why yes we do," said the commissioner.

"Then why has she been released?"

"Because she didn't kill your wife."

"Who did?"

"You did. Charles Elliot, you are under arrest for killing your wife, Margarita."

"That's preposterous!"

"No, as I said. We have all the proof."

The deputy stepped forward with handcuffs before Charles

could do anything. As Charles's mind raced with questions, he was fingerprinted, searched, and taken to a jail cell. How had they found out? This little village police commissioner couldn't have found out everything. He, Charles, was so much smarter than any cop. He would find a way out of this. After all, he always could talk or pay his way out of anything in the past.

As the deputy left him in the locked jail cell, he said, "If you have a lawyer, you'd better call him." And that was exactly what Charles intended to do as soon as possible.

CHAPTER 22

TRAIL'S BEGINNING

CHAPTER 22

TRIAL'S BEGINNING

"All rise! The court is now in session," stated the Sargent at Arms as the judge entered the courtroom.

The courtroom was packed. Sitting in the back row was Charles's mother, the Commissioner, Marielena, and Marielena's landlady, Señora Santiago. Sitting together in another row of the courtroom were Charles's household employees, Isa, the cook; Paula, the housekeeper; and Pedro, the gardener. Others in attendance were the many townspeople who had scrambled to fill all the remaining seats. Much of the press, some from as far away as Madrid, were left standing or sitting in the aisles.

Charles sat at the defendant's table with his lawyers, not one but two. They were the best money could buy. Both were nationally recognized as tough lawyers, who always got their clients' cases dismissed, sometimes over just a small technicality. They also usually won monetary awards for their clients for defamation of character, either from an adversarial client or the government itself.

Charles looked angry. He couldn't believe this was happening. Even though the commissioner had assured him that they had enough evidence to convict him, he couldn't imagine that it was true. He'd been so clever all of his life. And, he had been doubly clever in planning and executing his plan to kill Margarita. He had covered all of his tracks. No one had ever thought to question his actions or motives before. As he looked quickly around the courtroom, he saw his mother. Even though she had stayed after the funeral saying that she was there to comfort him in his loss, he now questioned her motives. What was she doing here? As he looked down the same row, he saw the commissioner, Marielena, and Señora Santiago. He couldn't escape the thought that he had all the evidence stacked against Marielena for the murder. Now, here she was, a spectator at HIS trial. She should be sitting where he now sat. Something was horribly wrong. In his anger, he mixed fact and fiction in his mind. She's guilty, not me, was his thought.

The three days between Charles's arrest and trial had been used for jury selection. From what Charles understood, the judge had experienced no difficulty finding people anxious to be part of the jury. Everyone knew this trial was the most important to ever occur in their little village and everyone wanted to be part of it. They knew if they were part of it, they'd be telling stories about it to future generations. Since Charles hadn't really made any friends of the townspeople, no one had claimed to have a bias for him. As for Margarita, she had made a number of friends in the Catholic church for her work with the children there. She was also a celebrity, having been Miss Spain. The townspeople were very happy to have someone to blame for her murder, but they really didn't know for sure if it had been her husband or someone else who murdered her. Many knew that Marielena had initially been arrested for the murder and then released. Many were anxious to hear the evidence against him, but during jury selection no one had claimed not to be biased against him.

The bailiff read the charges, "The village of San Anton, the City of Toledo, and the country of Spain against Charles Elliot for the murder of Margarita Elliot."

The judge looked down at Charles and asked him, "How do you plead?"

Charles glared back at the judge and yelled, "Innocent, obviously!"

The judge responded, "We need only a one-word answer. Señor Antones, please tell your client to answer questions without any embellishments."

The bailiff then told everyone to sit down.

The judge called on Prosecutor Fenada to deliver his opening statement.

Prosecutor Fenada stood, walked to the jurors' bench, and looking them straight in the eye started to speak. He spoke in a subdued voice that made everyone in the courtroom strain to hear his words. "The state will prove that Charles Elliot is guilty of killing his beautiful wife, the former Miss Balearic Islands, Miss Spain, and Miss World. The state will be presenting evidence of that guilt and the jurors need to render a guilty verdict after all the evidence has been presented and to assign appropriate punishment."

The judge then called on Charles's lawyers to deliver their opening statement. Señor Antones rose, looked at the jury, and addressed the courtroom very loudly and clearly, "Charles Elliott, the defendant is innocent. He was in England at the time the murder occurred. The defendant will prove his innocence in this case and the jurors need to render an innocent verdict, as well as render appropriate payment by the state to Charles Elliot for defamation of character in bringing a frivolous murder charge against him. Mr. Elliot is a respected member of society and a successful businessman in many countries; furthermore, he has no criminal record of any kind. He is not a murderer." Señor Antones sat down and smiled at his client as though Charles had nothing to worry about.

Prosecutor Fenada stood and stated, "The prosecution would now like to present into evidence the photos of the crime scene." The judge granted him permission. He signaled the court technician to dim the lights and to start the photo display. As the lights were dimmed in the courtroom. Prosecutor Fenada said, "Some of these photos may be too graphic for some of you, but you need to see the gruesomeness of the murder scene."

The first photo was shown on the screen in front of the courtroom as Prosecutor Fenada continued, "Margarita Elliott's throat was cut and then she was stabbed fourteen times." The courtroom was filled with gasps of horror. They knew she had been killed, but not so brutally. That fact had not been divulged before this moment. The prosecutor stated, "You will notice that there was blood and rainwater mixed all over the floor where she was found. If you look closely," he said using a laser to point to the spot on the screen, "there is a dagger also laying near her. That was the murder weapon." He then showed a second photo of a closeup of the dagger. Showing a third photo, he said, "Look closely at the tiles of the floor here where the amount of blood and water has puddled around the victim's body." The fourth photo was displayed as he continued, "please note that the shape of the wounds exactly matches the shape of the dagger." He used the laser pointer to point first at the wound closeups and then at the dagger which had been placed in the same photo. As he nodded to the court technician to turn off the photos and to turn on the lights again, the people all over the courtroom started to mumble and whisper to each other. Banging his gavel, the judge said, "The courtroom will come to order."

Prosecutor Fenada then stated, "The murder occurred on the night of April 22nd during the thunderstorms which inundated our village and her body was found by the household staff members. I call to the stand the housekeeper, Paula Zamora."

Paula was sworn in and sat in the witness box. She looked over at Charles and then quickly looked at the jurors. Many of the jurors were her friends whom she had grown up with. She had sworn to tell the truth and knew that her testimony was only the beginning of this ordeal. She had loved Margarita and wanted justice for her. The commissioner had told her not to discuss anything prior to the trial and she had complied. Now was her chance to speak.

The prosecutor asked, "During the night of April 22, did you hear any noises that would indicate that a murder might be happening?"

"No. All I heard was the storm," she answered.

"And the next morning. Did you hear anything unusual?"

"Yes. I was in the kitchen and heard a scream from the upstairs room which was being used as an art studio."

"What did you DO?"

"I ran upstairs and found Margarita dead on the floor."

"Was there anything next to her body?"

"There was Marielena, the artist, and a dagger."

"What did you think at that time?"

"That Marielena and Margarita had struggled and Margarita had screamed as Marielena had killed her."

"What made you come to that conclusion?"

"There was an enormous amount of blood on the floor."

"Was there anything else on the floor?"

"The floor had a lot of water on it too, mixing with the blood."

"Was the blood thick or thin?"

"Objection, Your Honor!" Yelled Señor Antones, Charles's lawyer. "The prosecution is leading the witness."

The judge looked at the prosecutor and said, "Please rephrase your question."

Prosecutor Fenada then asked, "What did the blood look like which was on the floor?"

"It was mixed with the water and looked thin."

"Was there anyone else with you at that time?"

"Yes. Isa Ortega, the cook, and Pedro Cordoba, the gardener."

"What happened then?"

"We grabbed Marielena and called the police commissioner."

"Why did you grab Marielena?"

"We assumed that she had killed Margarita."

"Thank you, that is all for now. I reserve the right to call this witness at a later time."

The judge then called for Señor Antones to cross examine.

Señor Antones rose and stepped up to the witness box.

He asked, "What was the relationship between Marielena and Margarita?"

"Marielena had been hired by Charles Elliot to paint Margarita's portrait. The relationship was a professional one. Not personal, but they did seem to get along well with each other."

"If I may ask, what was Marielena's relationship with Charles?"

"I'm not sure what you mean?"

"Were they more than employer and employee?"

"Not that I'm aware of."

"Did they seem to get along well with each other too?"

"From what I saw, yes."

"Could the relationship have been romantic between Charles and Marielena?"

"No, I never saw anything like that."

"But you never saw them anywhere other than in the studio where she was working?"

"No. Only in the studio, but there was nothing romantic between them because they didn't look at each other THAT way!"

"Are you sure?"

Prosecutor Fenada leaped to his feet as Paula answered this second insinuating question and said loudly, "The defendant's lawyer is coming to a conclusion without evidence. I move that his last two questions and answers be stricken from the record." Charles chuckled to himself. At least we've planted a little doubt.

The judge admonished Señor Antones and then told the jurors to disregard the last questions; however, they had already heard Paula's statement twice that there wasn't anything romantic between Charles and Marielena.

Señor Antones then said, "I have nothing further to ask this witness at this time."

The Judge dismissed Paula from the witness stand. He then asked the prosecutor to continue and Prosecutor Fenada called Isa

Ortega, Charles's cook, to the witness stand. As she was sworn in, Charles whispered to his lawyer, "What does she have to do with this trial?" His lawyer hushed him and watched expectantly.

Prosecutor Fenada asked her, "How long have you been employed at the villa?"

"Almost five years."

"Did you witness any kind of relationship between the deceased, Margarita, and the artist, Marielena?"

"Yes. I had on many occasions delivered drinks or lunch to the ladies in the studio as they worked."

"How would you describe their relationship?"

"They were often laughing and joking together. They seemed to enjoy each other's company."

"Even though Marielena was an employee?"

"Yes. They had grown quite close."

"What about the relationship between Marielena and the defendant, Charles Elliot?"

"At times it seemed that Marielena tried to avoid him, but she was always respectful."

"What about the relationship between Margarita and her husband, the defendant?"

"I've worked for many families over the years and seen many husband - wife relationships. Mr. and Mrs. Elliot sometimes had words with each other, but they didn't yell at each other the way some couples do. One tries to remain out of the relationships of one's employers; however, staff members cannot always shut their ears and not hear things. I believe that their relationship was strained, although Margarita remained the dutiful wife."

"On the night when Margarita was murdered, did you hear anything other than the storm?"

"No, sir. I didn't hear anything until the next morning when I heard a scream from the studio."

"Where were you at that time?"

"In the kitchen with Paula."

"Had either Marielena or Margarita had breakfast that morning?"

"No, and that was unusual. They tried to be at work in the studio by nine o'clock, but they always ate before meeting there."

"What did you do when you heard the scream?"

"I rushed to the studio upstairs."

"Can you describe what you saw at that time?"

"Both women were on the floor surrounded by blood and water. There was a dagger lying next to Margarita."

"What happened next?"

"I went to call the police commissioner, and Pedro and Paula held Marielena."

"What did you think at that time?"

"Even though I could scarcely believe it, I thought that Marielena had killed Margarita."

"Had you ever before seen the dagger that was on the floor next to Margarita?"

"Yes. It was the one that Mr. Elliot had Paula and me have sharpened by the scissors grinder and the one that was to be a prop in the portrait of Margarita."

"Where was Charles Elliot the night Margarita was murdered? And, where was Charles Elliot the morning that her body was found?"

"We had been told that he was on a business trip to England and would be returning in four days."

"Thank you. I have no further questions at this time. Prosecutor Fenada stepped away from the witness box, and Señor Antones rose from his seat next to Charles. As he moved toward Isa, he asked her, "Did you like your mistress, Margarita?"

"Oh, yes, sir. She was a lovely person."

"And what was your opinion of the defendant, Charles Elliot?"

"He was my employer."

"That's not what I asked. I asked your opinion of Charles Elliot."

"He was sometimes hard to talk to."

"Did you like him?"

"Objection," yelled Prosecutor Fenada. "The defense is asking a leading question concerning this witness's feelings. That is irrelevant."

The judge stated, "I agree. The jurors should disregard the last question." Charles thought, oh, that was good. We've established that she is against me and isn't a good witness.

Señor Antones, thinking that he had destroyed this witness, said, "I have no further questions for this witness." Isa was released by the judge and left the witness stand.

Prosecutor Fenada rose again and stated, "I call to the witness stand the villa's gardener, Pedro Cordoba."

Pedro was sworn in and the prosecutor asked him, "Where were you on the morning when Margarita's body was found?"

"Out in the garden, sir," he answered.

"Why had you gone there that morning?"

"Because of the storm the night before, I was checking the entire yard, gardens, and house to see if any damage had occurred during the night."

"Were you a witness to the murder scene?"

"Yes, when I heard the scream, I ran up the balcony steps and into the room."

"Were the balcony doors open at that time?"

"Yes, but the curtains were closed. I had to push them open in order to get into the room."

"Was that unusual?"

"Yes. Usually, especially in a storm, both the doors and the curtains are closed."

"And when you entered the room, what did you see?"

Chapter 22 - Trial's Beginning

"Margarita, Marielena, and a dagger were on the floor surrounded by blood and water."

"What did you do?"

"I helped Paula hold Marielena, and Isa called the police."

"What did you think at that time?"

"I thought that Marielena had killed my mistress."

"Let's go back to what you were doing that morning for the next question. On your inspection of the yard, grounds, and house that morning, did you see any damage or anything else that was different or stood out as unusual?"

"Yes. By the back gate of the garden, almost hidden under a bush, were tire tracks in the mud. The ground was extremely wet because of all the rain."

"Can you describe these tire tracks?"

"They looked to be of an old-fashioned bicycle, with fat tires."

"Were there any bicycles in the villa?"

"Not to my knowledge."

"Did you mention the tire tracks to anyone?"

"Yes. When the police commissioner, detective, and coroner were there, the police commissioner asked me the same question that you just did, and I told him about the tracks."

"What did you do then?"

"I took the commissioner out and showed him the tracks."

"Do you know if he did anything about the tracks?"

"Yes, he came back later and made plaster of paris impressions of them."

"And, you witnessed that?"

"Yes, sir."

"Were there any other things which you showed the commissioner at that time?"

"Yes. When we went into the garage looking to see if there

was a bicycle there, we found a pair of horned-rimmed glasses and a rubber glove near the trash can which is stored in the garage."

"Was anything done with those items?"

"Yes. The commissioner took them with him."

"What was your impression of the artist Marielena?"

"She seemed like a nice person."

"And of Margarita?"

"She was a lovely lady."

"And of the defendant, Charles Elliot?"

"He seemed to be a fair man, at least in his dealings with me."

"You don't live on the villa's premises, do you?"

"No, sir. I live in the village."

"So, you were not at the villa until the morning that the victim was found?"

"Yes, sir, I was not at the villa during the storm, I was in the village until that morning when I came up to the villa to start work."

"Thank you. That will be all for this witness at this time." Prosecutor Fenada walked back and sat down as Señor Antones walked forward to cross examine.

"When you came to the conclusion that Marielena had killed Margarita, did you question that conclusion?"

"No, sir. It looked like that was what had happened."

"Were you surprised?"

"Yes, sir."

"Why?"

"It seemed to me that they had gotten along fine with each other."

"Did it occur to you that the defendant, Charles Elliot had killed his wife?"

CHAPTER 22 - TRIAL'S BEGINNING

"No, sir. He was in England."

"Thank you. You are excused as I have no further questions."

Charles mused. Well, at least we're proving where I was. And, if I was in England, I couldn't have been in Spain killing my wife.

The judge, looking at his watch, called for a thirty minute recess and cleared the courtroom. While the judge left the courtroom, Charles turned to his lawyer and said that he thought he had done a good job in this first part of the trial. His lawyer said, at least we have shot down one witness that she didn't like you, we have proven where you were during the night of the murder, and we have everyone stating that you and your wife had a relatively peaceful marriage. I hope the rest of the trial goes as well. Then Charles and his lawyer separated as Charles was taken back to a cell in the courthouse.

When the courtroom reconvened, Prosecutor Fenada called Marielena to the witness stand. As she rose and came forward, Charles smirked to himself. Surely, they had to be kidding? What evidence could she possibly have against him? He knew he had placed enough evidence to convince anyone that she had done it, but what did she know? Stupid little back country artist! Almost as stupid as the commissioner and this "village idiot" of a prosecutor. This was going to be a fiasco.

Marielena was sworn in and then was asked by the prosecutor, "How did you become involved with the Elliotts?"

She stated, "I was sketching in the village one day and Charles Elliot commissioned me to paint his wife's portrait. He said that the portrait was to be a gift to his wife and would be presented to her at a celebration of her birthday."

"And you accepted the commission?"

"Yes, with the provision that he would pay half of the fee up front and pay the other half upon completion and acceptance of the portrait."

"And is it finished?"

"For all intents and purposes."

"Were there any other stipulations concerning the portrait?"

"Yes. It had to be done with her birthday as a deadline since there was to be a big celebration in which it was to be unveiled."

"So, you had to have it completed in a certain time frame?"

"Yes, in fact during the last three weeks, Charles Elliot arranged for me to live at the villa so that all my time would be spent in the painting of it."

"Does that mean that you were living in the villa the night that Margarita was killed?"

"Yes."

"During the night of the murder, did you hear anything other than the storm?"

'No. My bedroom was on the other side of the villa. And the storm was too loud."

"Where were you in the morning?"

"I was in my room. Because of the storm I had overslept and was anxious to get to the studio. There were only a few finishing touches yet to complete on the painting."

"Did you go to the studio immediately?"

"Yes. Usually I ate breakfast before going to the studio, but it was later than normal, so I went there first."

"And what did you find?"

"The studio was dark, the curtains drawn shut. As I rushed to open them, I slipped. The floor was wet. As I fell to the floor, I saw the body of Margarita and next to her was the dagger."

"What did you do?"

"I screamed."

"And then?"

Chapter 22 - Trial's Beginning

"Paula, Isa, and Pedro came, held me, and then called the police."

"What did you tell them?"

"I didn't kill her. But they didn't listen to me. They didn't believe me."

"Let's go in another direction now. What was your relationship with the defendant?"

"Purely employee-employer."

"Were you in love with Charles Elliot?"

"Absolutely not."

"And what was your relationship with Margarita Elliot?"

"She was my subject in the portrait which I was painting; but she was also a friend. We had gotten very close."

Señor Antones jumped to his feet and stated loudly, "The witness cannot prove this 'friendship'. With Margarita gone, she cannot herself authenticate this witness's conclusion of a valid friendship." Charles laughed inwardly. His lawyer was doing a great job.

The judge asked the prosecutor to continue his questioning. Prosecutor Fenada then asked, "Do you have any proof of your friendship with Margarita?"

"Yes. During our time together she told me about her marriage, her inability to have children, and her suspicions about Charles being unfaithful to her."

"Hearsay!" Shouted Señor Antones.

Prosecutor Fenada without looking the least bit ruffled then asked, "Do you have any concrete proof of the friendship, perhaps that she trusted you?"

"Yes. She gave me documents and photographs for me to hide in my apartment for her."

"Did you take them and hide them for her?"

"Yes. I did. After her death I gave them to the police."

"And what did these documents and photographs show?"

"They were evidence that proved Charles's infidelities and trysts."

Charles was dumbstruck. How had Margarita kept her suspicions to herself and acted like everything was wonderful between them? Where had she obtained the documentation? He couldn't believe that she had entrusted this little artist who was nothing to her. Even though his lawyers had whispered to him as he was brought into the courtroom that they had been supplied with documents and photos of him, he really hadn't paid much attention to what they had told him. He hadn't believed that any documentation of him had been kept by anyone, much less his wife. He watched as the prosecution then returned to his table, picked up a stack of papers which he showed to Marielena and asked, "Are these the documents and photos which Margarita gave you and that you gave me?"

Marielena looked through the documents and photos slowly and then answered, "Yes, sir."

Prosecutor Fenada then approached the bench and stated loudly. "The state requests that these documents and photos be placed into evidence against Charles Elliot as proof of motive in the murder of his wife. These documents and photos were supplied to the defense this morning to show good faith in this trial and to fulfill all requirements of the state."

The judge accepted the packet documents and photos and then asked the Prosecutor Fenada, "Are these documents available to show the jurors?"

Prosecutor Fenada stated, "Yes, Your Honor."

He was about to signal the court technician to again dim the lights and turn on the projector when Señor Antones yelled, "Objection. These items are not relevant to the trial." Señor Antones and Señor Pueda, Charles's second lawyer, had looked over the documents and photos quickly that morning and had decided that they would try anything they could to prevent them from being shown to the jury.

The judge looked down at the two attorneys for the

defendant and asked, "Why should the jurors be deprived from seeing any related information that pertains to this trial?"

"Because they are not relevant," stated both attorneys in unison.

The judge then turned to Prosecutor Fenada and asked, "Are these relevant?"

"Absolutely Your Honor," stated Prosecutor Fenada.

The judge then stated, "Prosecutor Fenada, please proceed."

As the lights dimmed and the photos were shown one by one, Prosecutor Fenada took his laser pointer and showed in the many documents the comparison of the dates of Charles's business trips and the dates of photos from tabloids and newspapers. Charles appeared with different women in most of them, but with the same woman in a few. In every one Charles was looking at each of the women with sultry looks that could only be described as almost lecherous. Again, the courtroom was filled with mumblings and whisperings. Again, the judge had to call the courtroom to order.

When the lights were again turned on, the prosecutor asked Marielena, "Do you know if Margarita showed these documents to anyone else?"

"She told me that she had spoken to Padre Juan and Pastor Luis."

"Hearsay!" Again yelled Señor Antones. At that point the judge said, "I would like this testimony to proceed."

Prosecutor Fenada then asked, "Do you believe that Charles Elliot killed his wife?"

"Yes."

Charles and his lawyer looked at each other. While this testimony didn't prove he was guilty of killing Margarita, it certainly gave a good motive. It was damning evidence of infidelity and proof of a marriage built on lies.

Prosecutor Fenada then stated, "I have several more questions for you concerning your commission to paint Margarita.

Were there any concerns which you had during the time you spent at the villa?"

"Yes, there weren't enough lights in the studio and there was no protection for the floor in case of paint spills."

"How were these problems rectified?"

"Charles brought in more lights, both to light Margarita and to provide light for my canvas and easel. Also, since there was no protection on the tile floors to prevent paint damage, I was told to go into the garage and get a tarp to cover the tiles."

"Did you do that?"

"Yes, I did. But something strange happened when I removed a tarp. There was an old bicycle stored under one of the other tarps."

"Can you describe it?"

"It was an old-fashioned bike, all scraped and rusted, with only patches of red paint. The wheels and tires were fat ones."

"Did you do anything with the bicycle?"

"No. I just covered it up again and took the one tarp upstairs to the studio."

"Did you mention the bike to anyone?"

"Only after the murder - to the police commissioner."

"Thank you. Another question. The dagger. I understand it was to be in the portrait of Margarita, is that correct?"

"Yes. That was strange too. Charles told me that it was one of Margarita's family's heirlooms. But when I asked her about it, she said that she had never seen it before Charles had brought in objects to be used as props in the portrait. Her family was too poor to possess anything as expensive as that."

"Do you know how your fingerprints came to be on this murder weapon?"

"Yes, when we were arranging the props, Charles had me place all the objects on the table, as he said, 'in an artistic way'".

"Last question for now - was there anything else about the

portrait that didn't seem right before the scheduled celebration?"

"Yes. Although there was to be a huge celebration and unveiling of the portrait for Margarita's birthday, I was never asked about a frame for the canvas. To my knowledge, a frame was never ordered for it. It was of such a size that a frame would have had to have been special ordered."

"As though Charles knew there would be no celebration?"

"Objection!" Shouted Charles's attorney. "The prosecution is leading the witness to make a conclusion."

The judge asked the jury to ignore the last question, but Charles and his lawyer knew that the damage had been done.

The prosecution then stated, "I have no further questions of this witness at this time. Since the day is late, I respectfully asked the court to adjourn until tomorrow morning."

The judge agreed and dismissed the court reminding them that the cross examination of the current witness, Marielena, would begin the next trial day.

Charles's attorneys looked at each other grateful that they would have a whole night to prepare for their cross examination. And it would probably be a whole night of preparation.

CHAPTER 23

SECOND DAY

CHAPTER 23

SECOND DAY

The second day of Charles' trial brought even more spectators. Not only were all the benches, aisles, and back wall filled, but the halls outside also contained many people who were not early enough to get into the courtroom. As the judge entered and the bailiff called the courtroom to order, the air was tense with excitement. The judge recalled Marielena to the witness stand and reminded her that she was under oath. He then reminded Señor Antones that he was to cross examine the witness, as though he needed to. The two defense attorneys and their sharpest junior partners had worked far into the night brainstorming ways to discredit Marielena as a witness. It was going to be a brutal day on the witness stand for her if they had their way of it. Marielena had practically slammed the door shut for their client with her testimony the preceding day. Señor Antones had to make sure that the jurors saw her as a liar who was out for personal gain, not an innocent artist who happened to be at the right place at the wrong time.

The judge asked, "Are you ready to begin, Señor Antones?"

"Yes, Your Honor. I have some small questions for this witness."

Señor Antones rose to his feet and with a smile, walked up very close to the witness stand, and asked her, "Did you ever question why the Elliots hired you to paint Margarita?"

"Yes, but I took Mr. Elliot at his word when he said that he liked the sketch which I had done in the café the day that I met him."

"You normally don't do portraits, is that correct?"

"Yes. I'm known more for landscapes and seascapes. I very

seldom do portraits."

"What made you accept the commission? Was it because of Charles himself? Were you physically drawn to him?" Señor Antones looked over at the jurors and smirked wickedly.

"No, sir. Not at all."

"Are you sure?"

Before Marielena could answer, Prosecutor Fenada shouted, "Objection. The attorney is badgering the witness on a topic already established. She has stated previously that she was not romantically involved with the defendant, Charles Elliot."

The judge then cautioned Señor Antones to continue, but with discretion.

Señor Antones then turned to Marielena and asked her, "You just moved here recently from Rhonda. Why did you move here?"

Marielena responded, "I couldn't make enough money from my art in Rhonda to work full-time at my art. I had to have part-time jobs in order to be able to eat and pay my rent. I thought I might do better here, closer to Toledo and Madrid."

"In other words, you were in financial difficulties?"

"Yes. But all my bills were paid and I didn't owe anyone anything."

"But you needed money?"

"Yes."

"And your family - couldn't they help you financially?"

The judge at this point stated, "Señor Antones, where are you going with these questions? Are they relevant to the trial at hand?"

"Yes, Your Honor. Please bear with me as these questions will show shortly that they are relevant."

The judge then asked Marielena to answer the question.

"No, my family is poor and cannot help me."

"Did you and Margarita share stories about your poor

families?"

"Yes, sir."

"And you saw how well she was living now being married to Charles?"

"Yes."

"And when you worked in the villa and later moved into the villa, did you also live well?"

"Yes, but - only as a guest."

"Would you have liked to live that way all the time - permanently?"

"I'm not sure what you mean?"

"With Margarita dead, you could have Charles all to yourself and live in the villa too."

"Objection!" Yelled Prosecutor Fenada. "The witness here is not on trial. Charles Elliot is. This witness has repeatedly stated that she has never had any interest in the defendant."

The judge again warned Señor Antones about his questioning.

Señor Antones then turned to Marielena and asked, "Is it true that you, not Margarita, compiled all the so-called evidence that the prosecution presented to the court yesterday?"

"Objection!" Shouted Prosecutor Fenada. "The attorney for the defense is leading the witness to make false statements to benefit the defense."

The judge turned again to Señor Antones and said, "This is the third time you've been warned. Either end your cross-examination or get to a point which we can all understand in terms of its relevance to the trial of Charles Elliot."

Señor Antones then ask Marielena, "Did you accept the commission because Señor Elliot offered you a huge sum of money?"

"No. I set the price, not him."

"So, you set a high price because you saw that he was

wealthy?"

"No. I didn't even know who he was when I met him."

"Didn't you see a way to get money, which you didn't have, by ingratiating yourself into a wealthy family when you started the commission and later began painting in the villa?"

"Objection!" Yelled Prosecutor Fenada. "Again, the defense is putting Marielena on trial, and not the defendant."

Señor Antones smiled and said, "Perhaps we should look at another view of your relationship with the defendant. Marielena, did you not meet Mr. Elliot in the village several times without his wife?"

"Yes, but we were discussing the portrait."

"And did he not drive you home several times?"

"Yes, but it was late, we had a long painting day behind us, and he knew that I was tired."

"And did he not come to your apartment several times to speak to you alone?"

"Yes, but I never let him come in."

"And didn't many people see you together in the village and near your apartment so that there was talk about you in the village, as a young woman with a married man?" As he asked this question, he leered at her with a knowing smile to the jury.

"Not that I know of."

"Let's backtrack and ask this then. If it was Margarita that got all the so-called evidence, where did she obtain it?"

Marielena answered, "From the library. Even when I was there, she made trips to the library."

"So, if we asked the librarian about it. Perhaps she could verify that?"

"I don't know, sir."

Charles thought to himself that he doubted that Margarita had made herself known to the librarian. She was such a private person. He doubted that they would be able to get the librarian to testify. He smirked to himself. Small town, small town people!

Señor Antones then asked, as if it were an afterthought, "Marielena, when you found the bicycle, why didn't you say anything about it and covered it up again?"

Marielena answered. "At that time the bicycle was insignificant. I assumed everyone knew it was there and it was covered up to protect it. Even though it looked to be beat up, it looked like an antique bicycle to me and could be expensive. Really, it was none of my business to question what the Elliots had in their garage. Therefore, I said nothing about it."

"And the dagger? You say that Charles told you that it belonged to Margarita's family. Could you have misunderstood what he said - that it belonged to Charles's family, not Margarita's?"

"No, sir. He specifically said, 'this dagger belonged to Margarita's grandfather and I want it in the portrait for sentimental reasons' for my wife. I didn't misunderstand him. I know what he told me."

"One last question - how do you know that no frame had been ordered for the portrait?"

Marielena answered, "Truthfully, I didn't know, but it would have had to have been special ordered, and well in advance of the celebration, because of its dimensions. Then it would have had to have been put on the canvas archivally, which is a delicate procedure, costly, and requires specific professional work by a framer. The Elliots wouldn't have wanted such an important painting to be handled in any other way. I believe that no one had ever been scheduled for the framing, nor the frame purchased. This much I do know and, since I knew when the celebration was scheduled, the time frame didn't allow any extra time to accomplish any of those things."

"No further questions for this witness."

Señor Antones had tried to raise questions in the minds of every person in the courtroom about Marielena's value as a witness and about her truthfulness, but he hadn't been very successful. Marielena had stayed consistent, even under quickly changing questions and persistent pressure. Her testimony had remained solid.

Charles looked over at his lawyer. He realized that however hard his attorney had questioned Marielena, she had been up to the hardest of questions. She hadn't been shaken. Charles was beginning to doubt his lawyer's abilities.

The judge asked that Marielena be dismissed from the witness stand and asked Prosecutor Fenada to call his next witness.

Prosecutor Fenada rose and said, "I call to the witness stand, Antonia Oso."

Antonia rose from her seat in the midst of the townspeople in the courtroom and walked slowly to the witness stand. She was sworn in and looked over at Charles. Charles couldn't figure out who she was nor why she had been called.

Prosecutor Fenada asked her, "Do you know the defendant, Charles Elliot?"

"No, sir."

"Did you know the victim, Margarita Elliot?"

"Yes, sir."

"And how did you know Margarita?"

"I'm the village librarian and she came into the library quite often."

"How long would you estimate that she had been coming to the library? In other words, about how long had you known Margarita Elliot?"

"I'm not sure, but I am sure that it was probably around a year or a year and a half."

"Did she make herself known to you?"

"Yes, I remember the first time she came in, she didn't have a library card - the library is free for all village residents, but you have to have a library card to check out books."

"And did she apply for a card then?"

"Yes, sir. She explained that as a child she had loved to read but hadn't done so for a long time. She said that her husband travelled and she had lots of spare time to read so she needed to have access to library books."

"Did she ask anything else?"

"At that time, she asked for recommendations of good books, which I was happy to give her. I read a lot myself so I know quite a lot of books to recommend."

"Did she come into the library quite often?"

"Yes, and she always made it a point to smile and wave to me at the desk, or to stop and talk quietly to me."

"So, you became a friend to the deceased?"

"Yes. That was why one morning when she came in, walked by the periodicals and tabloid section, and looked like she had seen a ghost, that I asked her if anything was wrong. She had turned white and was quite shaky. She had to sit down to seem to come to herself."

"And did she tell you?"

"Not fully, but later I put two and two together and realized what had happened."

"What did she do when you asked her what was wrong?"

"She asked if we had the ability in the library to copy materials. I told her that yes we did."

"And then?"

"She asked me where she could go to do that, and I showed her the area where our copy machines are located."

"Did she copy anything?"

"Yes, that day, but she came in the next day with some sort of list and asked if we could retrieve specific dated material - tabloids, periodicals, newspapers, and that sort of thing. At that time, I took her to the reading room and the storage rooms where we house recently published materials and back issues by date."

"About how often did she come in after that?"

"Quite often. She seemed to be looking for something every time she came in."

"Did you ever see what she was looking for?"

"Only once. She seemed to be extremely upset one day. She was trying to copy a tabloid photograph and was having difficulties with the copy machine. She came to me, almost in tears, and asked for my help which I gladly gave her. As she placed the material which she was copying in front of me, I saw what she was trying to copy. It was a picture of a man and woman at what looked like some sort of party."

"Did you recognize the man and woman?"

"Not the woman at all and not the man, at that time."

"Did you later recognize the man?"

"Yes, sir," she said, looking over at Charles. "It was Charles Elliot, the defendant. I later saw his picture in our village newspaper, as the husband of Margarita."

"So, you really didn't know at first what kinds of copies that Margarita was making?"

"No, sir. But she must have been gathering together all the evidence which you previously showed the courtroom about his infidelities."

"You're sure that that evidence was gathered by the deceased, and not the witness, Marielena?"

"Yes, sir. It was the wife, not the artist, who gathered the evidence."

"Could she have forged the picture of the defendant onto pre-existing material?"

"I know that young people these days who have lots of computer knowledge can do that, but our computers in the library don't have that capability; and I doubt that Margarita could have done that. She had trouble just running our copy machine." The spectators in the courtroom could be heard to laugh softly at the last comment.

"Thank you," stated Prosecutor Fanada. "Your witness," he said to Señor Antones.

Señor Antones rose, walked to the witness stand, and asked in cross-examination, "Antonia, had you ever met the defendant, Charles Elliot?"

"No, sir."

"So, you might not have been able to correctly identify him from what you saw that one day?"

"No, but I can identify him now. He's the man in all the evidence which his wife compiled. And, if she had all that evidence, he had a good reason to kill her."

At that the courtroom erupted in a bedlam of noise which the judge had to subdue with banging his gavel and shouting to bring the courtroom back to order. He again reminded the defense attorney to be circumspect in his questioning and the witness to stick to the questions asked.

At that Señor Antones said, "I have no further questions for this witness."

Prosecutor Fenada called Señora Sylvia Santiago to the witness stand. She stepped from her seat near Marielena and walked slowly down the aisle to the witness stand. Prosecutor Fenada helped her step up into the witness stand and she was sworn in.

His first question to her was, "How long have you known Marielena?"

"She has lived in my attic apartment for almost a year now."

"Do you know the defendant, Charles Elliot?"

"No, but I have seen him bring Marielena home from the villa, Marielena explained to me who he was, and I have seen him in the village."

Chapter 23 - Second Day

"Did you ever see him romantically involved with her?"

"No. Every time he was near my house, she came in quickly. She never ever invited him into the house."

"And how did you know that?"

"Because I'm somewhat of a busy body and am constantly looking out my windows at the neighbors. I've always watched Marielena." At her comment the townspeople started to laugh loudly.

The judge again reminded the courtroom that it had to maintain silence.

"And why did you particularly watch Marielena?"

"Because as a single woman, her actions had to be of such a nature that they didn't give her a bad name. That's true of all single women." With that comment, her neighbors in the courtroom could be seen to nod their heads in agreement.

"The defense attorneys have tried to question Marielena's character. What is your opinion of Marielena?"

"She is a fine upstanding young woman. She is trustworthy and fair in her dealings. She is circumspect in her relationships. And she pays her bills. She even paid all her rent ahead when she was given the commission down payment by Señor Elliot."

"You believe that she had no romantic relationship with the defendant then?"

"Yes, sir. She had no romantic relationship with him."

"I have no further question for this witness."

Señor Antones walked to the witness stand and, looking at Señora Santiago in a glaring fashion, asked, "Since you really don't know the defendant, by your own admission, how could you judge his relationship with Marielena?"

"I may not know him, but I know her."

"I have no further questions for this witness." Señora Santiago was told to return to her seat in the courtroom and the judge asked Señor Antones to return to his seat.

As he sat down, Prosecutor Fenada called Padre Juan to the witness stand. After his swearing in, the priest refused to answer the questions about talking to Margarita about her marriage. He stated that what information he had, concerning their marriage, had been obtained in Confession. He was bound by his spiritual oaths that Confessional information is confidential and cannot be divulged. He was not cross-examined, as he had really not testified, and he was quickly dismissed from the witness stand.

Prosecutor Fenada then called Pastor Luis to the witness stand. After being sworn in, Pastor Luis was asked by the prosecutor, "Did Margarita Elliot come to you to speak about her marriage?"

"Yes, she did. She had all kinds of documents - the ones which were previously shown to the jury - about her husband's infidelities."

"What was your advice to her at that time?"

"I told her to wait, gather more information, and to act as if everything in the marriage was fine. I also told her that if she needed to speak to me again, to come see me."

"And did she?"

"No. Within several weeks she was murdered."

"Did anyone else come to speak with you about this issue?"

"Yes. Police Commissioner Rivera."

"What did you say to him when he approached you?"

"I asked him if Margarita had been killed by her husband because of what she knew about him?"

The courtroom erupted in loud talking and boos. The judge had to again silence the courtroom and bring it back to order. He told the prosecutor to continue with his questioning.

Prosecutor Fenada then asked, "Was it your conclusion that Charles had killed Margarita?"

"Yes."

Prosecutor Fenada then stated, "I have no further questions for this witness."

As he sat down, Señor Antones jumped up and asked, "Have you ever had any chance to work with or to know Charles Elliot?"

"No."

"So your conclusion as to his guilt in this murder was based only upon your talks with his wife before her death? Could someone else have killed her to your knowledge?"

"My conclusion was based upon the evidence of his infidelities as shown to me by the deceased. I have, personally, never had any contact with Mr. Elliot. From the evidence Margarita had, I assumed that he had a perfect motive to kill her. But yes, someone else may have killed her. It just looked suspicious to me."

"Thank you. I have no further question for this witness." Señor Antones walked back to where Charles was sitting and thought to himself that he had at least made one witness state that someone other than Charles might have committed the crime. While it was a small step in the right direction, it may have placed some doubt in the some of the jurors' minds. This was not as easy a trial as Charles had led him to believe that it would be when he had agreed to defend him. This was developing into one of the hardest trials of his career. He knew that Charles was doubting his abilities, and, at this point, he was starting to doubt himself. He looked at the second defense attorney and together they realized they had another long night of preparation ahead of them.

The judge looked at his watch and announced that because of the late hour and another long day tomorrow of testimony, he would reconvene the trial the next morning. He banged his gavel and the courtroom was cleared.

CHAPTER 24

THIRD DAY

CHAPTER 24
THIRD DAY

On the third day of the trial the courtroom was again packed. After being called to order, the judge instructed Prosecutor Fenada to proceed with his case against Charles. The prosecutor stood, looked at the jurors, and then said, "Let's start today with a brief review of what has already been presented to you. The victim was murdered on April 22 during a tremendous thunderstorm which drowned out all noises which may have been generated by the murder. Her body was found the next morning by the artist, Marielena, who screamed when she saw the body. Her scream brought the house staff to the scene of the murder. Beside the victim was a dagger which had Marielena's fingerprints on it. Marielena has testified that the dagger was given, after being sharpened as testified by the cook and the housekeeper, to her to be placed as a prop for the portrait of the victim. Marielena also testified that she had seen a bicycle in the garage when she retrieved a tarp for the studio; however, no bicycle was found by Commissioner Rivera and the gardener, Pedro. However, on the morning when Margarita's body was found, the gardener found bicycle tracks beside the back gate to the villa. Marielena, as verified by the housekeeper, stated that no frame had been ordered for the portrait which was to be unveiled this week during a birthday celebration for the deceased. Marielena was initially accused of the murder but was released. Today we need to see the reasons for that and for the arrest of the defendant, Charles Elliot, the husband of the victim. As was testified by the staff and Marielena, Charles Elliot had told everyone that he was in England for a business trip during the days preceding the murder, the day of, and the day after the murder. We, the prosecution, will prove that he was not in England during that time, but came to Spain, murdered his wife, and went back to England to be there when he was informed of his wife's murder. The state calls Commissioner Rivera to the witness stand."

After Commissioner Rivera had been sworn in, Prosecutor Fenada asked, "When you and your detective arrived at the villa the morning that Margarita's body was found, what did you discover?"

"My detective and I discovered the body of Margarita Elliot lying on the studio floor covered in blood and water, with the artist Marielena and a dagger laying near the deceased, as described by all witnesses. Margarita and the dagger were still laying on the floor, but Marielena was being held by two of the staff until I arrived. I have previously shown several photos of the crime scene to the jury."

"And what, at that time, did you assume?"

"That Marielena had killed Margarita."

"Was there anything about the scene which didn't correspond to that conclusion?"

"After a thorough examination of the scene, several things didn't add up."

"Such as?"

"First, Margarita's body was too cold to have just been killed. Second, there had been no other sound but the one scream. With the amount of blood present, there would have had to have been a struggle or fight, which usually makes more noise than one scream. Third, the blood was mixed with an enormously large amount of water - rainwater from the night before. Fourth, the curtains had been drawn, but the door to the balcony was still open - who closed the drapes - had it been the killer? Fifth, neither Margarita nor Marielena had eaten breakfast, as testified by the cook. It appeared that both of them had gone to the studio first thing in the morning, which according to the staff was unusual. They usually met at the studio at nine o'clock after both of them had eaten their breakfast. Sixth and lastly, in speaking to the gardener, he had seen unusual tire prints from a bicycle near the back gate."

"And what were your conclusions then?"

"Even though it looked initially like the murder had just occurred and that Marielena had committed the murder, it didn't add up. With the body that cold, the murder hadn't been just committed. It had been done sometime during the night when everyone was asleep. The blood hadn't congealed because of the rainwater which had diluted the blood, again during the night. If Margarita hadn't screamed as she was killed, then Marielena, who stated that she had screamed when she discovered the body, was the only scream which the staff heard. With the door open and the drapes closed, someone else had closed the drapes but had left the door open during the night. Probably the killer. And, finally, consider the tire tracks at the back gate. There might have been someone else, using a bicycle for transportation, who had committed the murder."

"Were you aware that Marielena was living in the villa at the time of the murder?"

"Yes. Several sources, the staff and Marielena herself, told me that she had been asked to live there until the portrait was completed."

"Yesterday the gardener also testified that after the murder, he and you also discovered a rubber glove and a pair of horned-rimmed glasses in the garage as well as the bicycle tracks."

"Yes, that is true."

"At that time could you determine to whom the glasses and rubber glove belonged?"

"No. The gardener, housekeeper, and the cook had never seen either of the items before."

"I see. And what did you do?"

"We took plaster of paris and made a permanent impression of the bicycle tracks and took the other two items with it to the police station as possible evidence."

Chapter 24 - Third Day

"I'll ask again. Were you having serious doubts about the guilt of Marielena at that time, even though you arrested her?"

"Yes. The staff seemed so sure that she had committed the murder; and, indeed, the scene and the preliminary evidence certainly made it look as though she had committed the murder, but it didn't add up."

"Now let's get this straight. You found bicycle tracks, but no bicycle at that time?"

"Yes."

"When were you aware that there had been a bicycle in the villa?"

"When I questioned Marielena at the police station."

"What was your next step?"

"I tried to put myself in the shoes of the murderer. I asked myself, if I were the murderer, where would I have gone after committing the murder."

"And did you come up with an answer?"

"Yes. The obvious escape route from the villa would have been to exit through the gate, go down the alley, and go into the village where I believed the murderer either had a car in which to escape or had taken a bus, a taxi, or the train."

"Did you pursue these avenues of thought?"

"Yes. By guessing the time of the murder, based upon Margarita's cooler core body temperature and the fact that rigor mortis hadn't completely set in yet, I could estimate a window of time in which the murderer committed the murder and exited the scene. Rigor mortis usually sets in between two and six hours under normal room temperature. Margarita's body was found before nine in the morning, but it was not at normal room temperature. There was a cooler than normal ambient temperature in the room due to the lowered temperature caused by the thunderstorm that night and the drapes being closed. Furthermore, her body was lying on a cold tile floor and in pooled water. I estimated time of the murder was between 2 AM and 4

AM. It couldn't have been later than that or the murderer could not make an exit without being seen by someone and it couldn't have been much before that time or the murderer would again have risked being seen. It was almost exactly the time when the worst of the thunderstorm was occurring."

"Did you trace your supposed means of exit?"

"Yes. There were no taxis, buses, nor car rental agencies available at that time of morning; and, with parking in the village at a premium, I assumed that a private car was out of the question. I then looked at the train schedules. The first train from Toledo to Madrid was an option for the murderer, but the murderer would have to get there. A bicycle seemed a good bet. What streets would the murderer have to travel was my next question. I, therefore, walked from the back gate of the villa, down into the village. As I crossed the bridge at the river, I thought that would be a good place to ditch the bicycle. Looking down, I discovered a bicycle partly concealed by debris from the storm's waters."

"Did you go down and look closer at the bicycle?"

"Yes. And what was amazing, the bicycle matched the description which Marielena had given me of a bicycle which she had seen in the villa's garage when she went for a tarp. My deputy and I retrieved the bicycle and matched its tires to the plaster of paris impressions which we had taken from the garden. If you please, Your Honor, I would like to place in evidence that same bicycle and the plaster of paris impressions." At that point, the deputy went out and brought in the bicycle and the impressions and presented them to the judge. The courtroom erupted in whispers and talking. Everyone in the courtroom strained in their seats as the old bicycle was wheeled in and a large wooden plank with the plaster of paris impression was delivered to the front of the courtroom. The judge banged his gavel to restore order. Señor Antones rose and said, "Judge, I must protest. This is all speculation on the commissioner's part. I see no relevance to this trial."

Chapter 24 - Third Day

The judge, looked at Prosecutor Fenada and stated, "Please stick to the important points of the trial."

Prosecutor Fenada stated, "Sir. All of this information IS relevant which will be momentarily demonstrated."

The judge then said, "Please proceed then."

Prosecutor Fenada asked the commissioner, "Was there any other evidence which had been found under the bridge?"

"Unfortunately, no. The flood waters must have swept away anything else which had been thrown off the bridge." Charles mused to himself, at least the bag of clothes and the other rubber glove had not been found. Good.

"Commissioner, did you try to trace the bicycle in any way?"

"Yes. I started looking for a pawn or second-hand shop that might have sold such a bicycle."

"Did you find one?"

"Yes, and I got both a receipt and a description of the man who purchased the bike. I offer both of these in evidence here." He handed the Sargent-at-arms the two items.

The prosecutor then asked, "What did you do in tracing the pathway of the murderer?"

"I assumed that the murderer, after throwing the bicycle from the bridge, was now on foot. There were no trains at that time of morning to get to Toledo, but the walk there from our village isn't all that strenuous. I went the next morning to Toledo at the time of the first train to Madrid and questioned the regular commuters about anyone unusual or anything out of the ordinary which they might have seen the morning after the big storm."

"Were you able to find any witnesses who saw anyone?"

"Yes. And they gave me a very detailed description of a man who was unknown to them, whom they had not seen before, and who was carrying a very large backpack. They described how he had gotten on the train with them, stayed to himself, and disembarked in Madrid. Two of my witnesses said that as soon as he reached the Madrid train station, he had gone into the men's room. Your Honor, I wish to present into evidence these affidavits from these witnesses at the Toledo train station."

"Before we proceed further here, let me ask you about these descriptions, one from the shop owner and the other from the commuters. Did these descriptions match?"

"No. But I guessed that perhaps two persons might have been involved or that different disguises might have been used by the same person. At that point, I wasn't sure which was the correct assumption. I decided to follow the description from the commuters and go to Toledo and take the chance that perhaps the train station's security cameras could have video of the man and confirm the commuters' description of the suspect and what he did there. There was a possibility that I had missed something so I went to Toledo. We have some video which we need to have entered into evidence as to what I discovered in Toledo."

The judge said, "I will allow them, if they are relevant."

"Yes, Your Honor, they are relevant."

"Objection" stated Señor Antones.

"Overthrown," stated the judge. "I'm very interested in seeing them, as I'm sure the jurors are."

Charles slumped forward in his chair and put his hands, which were now very white, up to his head. How had he been so stupid? But maybe it wasn't yet all lost. He thought of the backpack and its contents safely hidden in his bedroom at his parents' mansion. He would have to get there somehow and get rid of all that stuff as soon as he could. He had no reason to believe that any of it would have been found. Surely this bumbling commissioner, who seemed to ramble from one topic to another, wouldn't have gone to England. There was still hope. He straightened himself and took a deep breath.

The judge continued by saying, "Prosecutor Fenada, please proceed."

Chapter 24 - Third Day

"Now, if you can please explain this first video Commissioner."

"As I stated previously, after speaking to the commuters and getting a description of the unknown man on the train from Toledo to Madrid on the morning in question, I went to the train station, got permission to look at their security cameras, and found the same suspect in question on their videos. He boarded the train as the commuters had described. The next day I took the train to Madrid and went to their station master, obtained permission to view their security cameras, and again found the man. He went straight from the train to the men's room as described; however, he didn't come out. A man, looking different, but carrying the same backpack left the men's room. Please show the next video. As you can see, the backpack and his shoes are the same, the disguise is different, and - watch - he goes from one trash can to another and deposits something, leaving the sack which had contained the items in a separate trash can. If we follow the next video, the suspect then purchases another train ticket and boards the train from Madrid to Paris. What is interesting about the disguises, the man's appearance has been altered and he has on different clothing, but he's wearing the same shoes and carries the same backpack."

"What did you do then Commissioner?"

"I went to Paris and followed the same procedure there. I contacted the authorities in the train station, obtained permission to see their security videos, which have also been placed in evidence with the other videos. Please see on the next video, this person continued the same process as had happened in Madrid. Again, he has the same shoes and backpack, but a different disguise. This time our suspect took the fast train to London from Paris."

Charles although sitting extremely still was beginning to feel that his world was crumbling. How could this small town, poor excuse of a policeman, have tracked him down? At least he probably didn't know about all the things in the closet of the mansion. At this point even his lawyer was glancing at him sideways.

The prosecutor stated, "What else should we see here?"

"Please note, the man's size and shape in all these videos are the same. The shoes are the same and the backpack is the same," stated the commissioner. "Now show the videos from the London train station."

As everyone in the court strained to see the screen, the video from London showed the man, who had gotten on the train in Paris, came off the train with the same backpack and shoes went into the men's water closet. A very short time later the man who emerged from the men's water closet, carrying the backpack, and wearing the same shoes was Charles Elliot. The courtroom erupted in loud voices.

"Order in the court," yelled the judge. "Would the prosecutor and the defense lawyer please approach the bench?" Both did. Looking at the prosecutor, the judge asked, "Is this the end of your surprises?"

"No, Your Honor. We have more - at least another day's worth of testimony from several more witnesses."

"And, what about the defense?"

"We haven't even begun yet to try to defend, and that's at least another day," replied Charles's lawyer.

At that the judge dismissed them to their seats; and, addressing the courtroom, stated, "This trial is in recess until tomorrow. I would remind everyone here that I will not tolerate another outburst like this one that has just occurred. You're dismissed."

Charles's lawyer looked at him and quietly stated, "I hope that you can explain this. We need to talk about the evidence that has just been presented against you. You swore to me that you were innocent when I took this case. I'm beginning to doubt your word. Tomorrow I have to cross examine this policeman, but it seems he has plenty of evidence against you." Then he let the deputy take Charles back to his cell.

CHAPTER 125

FOURTH DAY

CHAPTER 25
FOURTH DAY

As everyone gathered together in the courtroom for the fourth day of the trial, the mutters of all present sounded like a beehive. Again, every seat was occupied and the crowd of spectators spilled out into the hallway outside the courtroom. The preceding day's revelations were on every mind. As the judge and bailiff entered, the noise level dropped almost immediately.

"Thank you," said the judge. "I caution you again that you must maintain silence today or risk the courtroom being cleared of all spectators. Could the prosecutor please continue with the witness, Commissioner Rivera."

Prosecutor Fenada stood, reminded the commissioner that he was under oath, and asked, "Commissioner, after discovering that the suspect you were following appeared to be the defendant, Charles Elliot, what did you do?"

"I went to the Elliot mansion outside London, introduced myself to Lady Elliot, and spoke to her as Lord Elliot is in poor health and was asleep when I arrived there."

"And do you see her here in the courtroom?"

"Yes. She is sitting in the back of the courtroom as we speak."

All of a sudden Charles realized why his mother was in the courtroom. No, he thought, not my own mother against me. I have been so careful throughout all the years. I know that I've always fooled my parents. Of course, she'll be on my side. How could she not?

The prosecutor looked at the judge at that point and indicating Commissioner Rivera, he said, "I reserve the right to recall this witness at a later time; however, at this time I would like to call Lady Anne Elliot to the witness stand."

The judge responded, "As you wish. Commissioner Rivera please step down, and Lady Anne Elliot, please come forward and be sworn in."

After the commissioner and Lady Elliot exchanged places, and, after Lady Elliot was sworn in, the prosecutor began by asking her, "Are you the mother of the defendant, Charles Elliot?"

"Yes, I am," she replied.

"I understand that you met Commissioner Rivera at your home several weeks after your daughter-in-law's murder?"

"Yes. He came to our home, introduced himself, and explained that he was investigating our dear, Margarita's murder."

"Did he ask you about Charles's marriage to her?"

"Oh, yes, and I said that there had been problems." She quickly rhetorically added, "All marriages have problems, don't they?" Then she paused and added, "Margarita was unable to conceive a child, but Charles had told her that he would try to find an adoption agency where they could adopt a child or children."

"And did he do that?"

"To my knowledge, he didn't as they never adopted nor even started the procedure to adopt."

"What did he do?"

"What do you mean?"

"Did he continue in his marriage like before?"

Glancing quickly at her son she said very quietly, "I don't think so. I think he tried to make it look like he did, but he continued going on business trips and other engagements."

"Can you explain that more fully?"

"I know of at least one occasion, and there were probably more, when he was in England and he spent a lot of time with a woman he met at the Prime Minister's."

"Of the photos and dates exhibited here previously, did you recognize this woman?"

"Yes. She was the blond in the emerald green dress in the one photo."

"And, you have reason to believe that Charles and this woman were close, maybe even romantically involved?"

"I have it on a very reliable source that they became intimate the very night when they met. You see, I found out about it through a family friend, and then I, without my husband knowing, followed up with a series of phone calls to several other people whom I know who live at One Aldwyah in Covent Gardens. It was the first of several times they spent nights there together."

Charles glared at his mother. How could she? He thought of how his father had hoodwinked his mother for years and how for years he had hoodwinked both of them. What had changed? How could he have let this happen?

"Objection," stated his lawyer, "do you have proof of this?"

"Yes," said Lady Anne. She removed some papers from her handbag and gave them to the prosecutor, who, after looking at them, in turn passed them to the judge stating, "The prosecution wishes to have these papers entered as evidence." Charles's mother had hoped that she wouldn't need those papers. As she had watched her son during the three days of the trial and seen his smug smile, she was glad that she'd brought them. Even her husband didn't know that she had them. Her friends had convinced the manager of the London hotel to give her notarized copies of registrations and copies of their security camera photos showing Charles and Lady Louise together.

Prosecutor Fenada then asked her, "Returning to the day that Commissioner Rivera came to your home, what did you and he discuss besides Charles's marriage to Margarita?"

"We discussed the days before and after Margarita's death and Charles's activities during that time." A tear appeared in her eye and rolled down her cheek.

"Did he accuse your son of the murder at that time?"

"No, not at first. He asked where Charles had been during

the time that he was in England. He said that the staff in the villa had said that Charles was in England on a business trip."

Oh, yeah, Charles thought. Now she'll give me my alibi that I made sure to have.

The prosecutor continued, "And, did he go to his apartment in London or did he stay at your home?"

Charles almost jumped up in surprise. How did the commissioner know about his apartment in London?

Lady Anne said, "He stayed with us, but he went into the London office every day that he was there. He was complaining of not feeling well. The night of Margarita's murder, he had said that he was going to take a sleeping pill and try to sleep off whatever was bothering him."

The prosecutor asked, "Did he?"

"That's what the commissioner asked me," she said. "I accused the commissioner of thinking that Charles had killed her; and, when I did, he answered that he had in his possession a number of items that made him think that Charles was not at our home the night that Margarita was murdered."

"Did he show you those items?"

"No, but he asked me if there were any strange things that I could remember which happened that night."

"And did you?"

"Yes, I described seeing a strange man in the yard, about the same size and shape of my son, who looked like he was walking toward our garage. By the time I summoned the gardener and he went to look for the man, he had disappeared."

"Did he look familiar, this man that you saw?"

"It's funny, he looked a little like my son, but he had long grey hair and was wearing glasses. The man walked mostly in the shadows. It was late evening and we were at dinner."

"Did you hear anything from your son's room during the night?"

"No, but I didn't expect to. After all, he had said he was taking a sleeping pill and was not to be disturbed. He was going to 'sleep off' whatever was making him feel ill."

"What time did Charles get up the next morning?"

"He didn't. He came down shortly after noon and said he felt much better. He said he was glad that he had slept soundly all night."

"What happened then when you talked to the commissioner?"

"He asked to see Charles's room. He said that he could obtain a search warrant and come back later if I had any objections. She paused and then continued, "At first, I hesitated. Then I relinquished, knowing that if I refused, he would think that I had something, or rather Charles, had something to hide. I didn't want to postpone the search, because, if I did and there was a search later and nothing was found, I didn't want the commissioner to think I had destroyed any evidence in the interim. I really didn't think he'd find anything, so I gave him permission to search Charles's room. In fact, I offered to help him. I still believed my son was innocent."

"What happened when you and the commissioner went to Charles's room?"

"The first thing we looked at was the window to Charles's room. The tract had been greased. It made absolutely no sound when you opened and closed it. Underneath the window were large vines, some of which had torn branches." At this point the prosecutor took some photos and entered them into evidence.

"Did you notice anything else concerning this window?"

"Yes, if you were to go down to the ground from that window, it was on the same direct pathway from the house to the garage, the same line that I had seen the stranger walk the early evening of the night that Margarita was murdered."

"Do you know if Charles could have driven his car out of the garage? Did you see or hear his car leave?"

"No. I don't think so. He has a sports car and the sound is quite distinctive."

"Then what did you and the commissioner do?"

"After I came to the realization that perhaps my son had really killed his lovely wife, I suggest to the commissioner that we search the entire room together. We looked in everything, dressers, closet, the adjoining bathroom, under the bed, and everywhere."

"And what did you find?"

"A huge backpack with a number of items in it."

The prosecutor looked up at the judge and said, "We now have that backpack and the items to enter into evidence, Your Honor." At which time the prosecutor signaled the deputy to go out and bring in the huge backpack. Then he turned to the jurors and the courtroom and stated, "We have taken the liberty to photograph all the items which were found in this backpack and submit those photographs into evidence", he continued as he handed them to the judge. We will be showing those photos to you as needed throughout the trial."

The judge answered, "Evidence accepted. Please continue, Prosecutor Fenada."

Charles was thunderstruck. He jumped to his feet and yelled "That backpack isn't mine. This is a fabrication. I never saw that backpack in my life."

The judge banged his gavel and told the defense lawyer to control his client. The courtroom erupted in loud voices. Again, the judge banged his gavel and called the courtroom to order.

Prosecutor Fenada said to the jurors, "Please note that in this backpack were four passports with accompanying credit cards. I will match the passport photos to photos of the suspect in various train stations from the videos which were previously shown to you." When he got to the photo of the grey-haired and plastic glasses passport photo, he stopped and asked Lady Anne, "Do you recognize the person in this photo?"

"Yes," she answered. "That's the man I saw in the yard, the early evening that Margarita was killed."

Then the prosecutor asked her what she and the commissioner had done after they had discovered all the passports, credit cards, backpack, and the last clothing."

"We went to Charles's apartment in London, and later we went to the Elliot business office building."

"And what did you discover there?"

"In the apartment we found women's clothing that would never have fit my daughter-in-law, and at the office we viewed another security video of the office's underground parking facility."

The prosecutor took a deep breath and then said, "Please roll the last video which we presented into evidence. Please note the date that appears on this video. Like all the other security videos shown, the dates tell the story."

As the video ran, everyone in the courtroom witnessed the blatant lie that Charles had just yelled, for there was Charles getting into his car with a briefcase and the same backpack that had just been submitted in evidence. The prosecutor then showed Charles's photo again of him exiting the London train the morning after Margarita's murder carrying the same backpack again to emphasize his point.

The judge then asked, "Do you have anything further to add?"

Prosecutor Fenada then said, "No, Your Honor. I am finished with this witness."

Señor Antones rose slowly and approached the witness box. As he did so, he asked Lady Elliot, "Why did you help the commissioner search your son's room? You know that you weren't required to do so."

Lady Elliot replied, "At first I didn't think we would find anything so it would be safe for me to do so to show Charles had nothing to hide. After thinking, I realized that my dear Margarita needed to be remembered as she was, a wonderful woman who loved and trusted my son completely. I was not aware that he had defied her love. I believed she needed to be avenged. Her murder was a senselessly brutal murder; and, if my son had done it, I owed it to her memory to help bring her killer to justice. Even if it was my son."

Señor Antones slowly nodded his head and said, "I have no further questions for this witness."

Prosecutor Fenada stated, "I would like to recall Commissioner Rivera to the stand."

Lady Elliot was dismissed to her seat in the back of the courtroom and Commissioner Rivera retook the witness stand.

Prosecutor Fenada asked, "After you had spoken to Lady Elliot, what did you do then?"

"I returned to Spain with all the evidence. I searched for the order for a frame for the picture and I looked for the sale of the bicycle and the sale of the dagger."

"And how did those searches progress?"

"As you have seen the frame had never been ordered. We enlarged our search area to a 200-kilometer diameter around the villa and there had been no orders. As presented in evidence prior, the sale of the bicycle bore fruit as shown by the receipt of the sale and the description of the person purchasing it matches the one disguise of a black-haired man with horned-rimmed glasses and a mustache. As for the dagger, even though it is an expensive dagger, we were unable to find where it had been purchased; however, please remember that Charles had presented the dagger to the housekeeper and cook to have it sharpened; and had given it to Marielena to have it used as a prop in the portrait. He also lied to her as to its origin. It had not been in Margarita's family heirlooms as he professed."

The judge asked the prosecutor, "Do you have any other questions for this witness?" Prosecutor Fenada stated, "No, Your Honor."

Then the judge stated, "I am adjourning the trial at this point as the hour is late. We will begin the trial tomorrow with the cross-examination of this witness by the defendant's lawyers. You are dismissed."

CHAPTER 26

TRIAL'S END

CHAPTER 26

TRIAL'S END

The expectant crowd in the courtroom watched anxiously as the judge gaveled the court into session on the fifth day. Commissioner Rivera again took the witness stand but this time he was approached by Charles's lawyer, Senor Antones.

Señor Antones asked the commissioner, "When you went into the mansion in England, did you already know that Charles Elliot was guilty of the murder?"

"Yes, but I needed more evidence."

"Did you obtain a search warrant?"

"No. At first, I was only going to speak with Charles's parents. Also, since I'm not a policeman in England, I would have had to get their permission and their search warrant before conducting a search."

"But you searched anyway, without a warrant."

"Yes. Lady Anne volunteered that I search and offered to help me search."

"So, it was an illegal search of the premises."

"Objection," yelled Prosecutor Fenada. "The witness, Lady Anne Elliot, told the court that she had decided to let the search proceed without a warrant. She said that she thought that Charles had nothing to hide; and, if she refused to comply with a search, it would look as though her son was guilty and wanted to hide something. Or, if it took longer, it would look as though, if there was evidence, it had been destroyed, before a search. She even volunteered to help the commissioner search. We therefore have two witnesses that have testified that the search was done WITH permission."

"Duly noted," stated the judge. "The jury will disregard the insinuation by Señor Antones that the search at the mansion was illegal. Please continue your cross examination, Señor Antones."

Señor Antones looked at the judge and asked him, "Your Honor, may I have a few minutes to speak privately with my client?"

The judge stated, "This is highly irregular; however, in this instance, I grant a 30 minutes recess for you to do so."

The courtroom was abuzz with conversation. Charles and his lawyer and the bailiff went into the side room of the courtroom to talk. When they reached the room, Charles's lawyer looked at his client and said, "You lied to everyone, including me. How could you have hoped that I could defend you when, by the evidence presented, you made so many mistakes in killing your wife? I can't defend you against the insurmountable evidence which the prosecution has delivered. They have proven beyond an inkling of shadow of a doubt in the jurors' minds that you murdered her. I think your only recourse is to change your plea to guilty and hope the jurors will give you some sort of leniency. What were you thinking?

Charles looked up at him and said, "Yes. I'm guilty. I thought I could get away with it. I had no idea that they would have all this evidence. I thought I was dealing with ignorant people who wouldn't work so hard to get all the facts. Even my own mother helped them."

"Your arrogance is your Achilles Heel, Charles," said his lawyer. "I tried to get you off on the technicality of the commissioner not having a warrant to search the mansion, but it wasn't enough. Now my only course of action is to try to get your sentence reduced. Let's go back into the courtroom and I'll do my best."

As they entered the courtroom and everyone took their seats, the judge asked, "Señor Antones, do you have any further questions for this witness?"

Señor Antones stated, "I have no further questions, Your Honor." The judge then dismissed Commissioner Rivera from the witness stand. Looking at the prosecution, he said, "Will the Prosecutor present his closing arguments, please."

Prosecutor Fenada rose, looked at the jury, and walked over to the jurors' stand. He said, "I only have a brief summary. Security videos, witnesses' accounts, passport photos, and documents, given to Marielena by the deceased, have verified the following fact - Charles Elliot killed his wife, Margarita Elliot. Charles Elliot was NOT in England, but in Spain the night his wife was murdered. In fact, he not only was there, but he had a motive. He was married to a beautiful, but barren, woman who suspected his infidelities, a woman who had befriended, trusted, and confided in the artist who had been hired to paint her portrait. Charles Elliot, the defendant, had placed enough false evidence to frame this same artist for the murder while carrying out the deed himself. Because of his wife's relationship with the artist, the artist was able to exonerate herself, and to put the real murderer in a position of suspicion with Commissioner Rivera. The prosecution rests its case and charges the jury to bring in a verdict of guilty. Remember that there should be no suspicion of doubt in your mind. Charles Elliot is a murderer."

The judge then looked at the defendant and his lawyers. He said clearly, "Does the defense have a closing statement?"

Señor Antones rose, looked down at his client and then at the jury. "My client would like to say a few words to the jury before they bring in a verdict." Then he sat down and Charles stood up. With a trembling voice, Charles stated clearly, "I wish to change my plea to guilty. I'm truly sorry for all the pain which I have inflicted on my wife, my family, and everyone who trusted me." With that he sank back down in his seat.

Señor Antones again stood and said, "I plead with the jurors to consider these last remarks by the defendant and to take those in consideration both in their decision of guilt and the possibility of punishment." Then he again sat down.

The judge stated, "This court is adjourned until the jurors have reached their decision. Will the jurors reach a decision of innocence or guilt; and, if guilty, a decision as to the proper punishment."

The jurors filed out of the courtroom as did everyone else. No one left the courthouse. People stood in the hallway, on the sidewalks, and even in the street. Everyone was afraid that they would miss the end. As most assumed, it didn't take the jury long to reach a decision of guilt or innocence. It was the decision of punishment that took the longest.

Unbelievably the jurors were only in their quarters for four hours until they asked to reconvene in the courtroom. As everyone came in to be seated, Marielena held hands with Charles's mother who had made every attempt to apologize for her son's behavior toward her.

The judge asked the jurors, "Have you reached a decision of guilt or innocence?"

The foreman of the jury replied, "Yes, Your Honor, we have," he paused, "we find the defendant, Charles Elliott, guilty of the murder of his wife, Margarita Elliot. This decision was made easy by the defendant changing his plea to guilty."

"And, have you made a decision as to his punishment?"

"Yes. In light of the premeditated and vicious nature of the murder, we have come to the decision that Mr. Elliot should have a life sentence with no opportunity of parole. The decision of punishment was the most difficult to determine, especially since the defendant has now changed his plea and professed remorse. Many of the jurors wanted the death sentence; however, our conclusion rests in the fact that he will have the rest of his life to think about the seriousness of his crime and their consequences on everyone concerned."

The judge thanked the jurors for their work during the past week. He thanked both the prosecution and the defense team as well. Then he adjourned the courtroom.

Charles's mother watched as he was taken from the courtroom. He looked back at her and saw that she was weeping.

Marielena and Commissioner Rivera left the courtroom together. He asked her about her plans.

"Since I have no money, I will have to go back to what I was doing prior to this commission work. I'll start painting and sketching in the village again."

He asked, "What was the contract like that you signed with Charles for Margarita's portrait?"

"The contract stated that he would pay me half down, which he did, and the final half would be paid upon completion of the painting, if he approved of it."

"And is it finished?"

"Yes, but with the circumstances the way they are, I'm sure that Charles doesn't want a painting of the wife he murdered." She paused and then added, "It looks like I'm the owner of this huge painting. I'm not sure what will happen to it. Charles's mother stated that she and her husband really don't want it either as there would be too many bad memories. Lady Elliot said that because of its large size, they would move it for me to wherever I'd like it. They'll be selling the villa and emptying out all the contents there. I really don't have room for it in my attic apartment. So - I don't know what I'll do."

"Why don't you let me store it for you in the police station for a while. We have a huge storage room that we could place it in for a short time. That would give you a little time to decide what to do with it."

"Oh, that would be very kind."

"I'll see to it that it will be brought by my deputy and stored for you."

"Thank you," she said as they separated in the street. "I'll think about it and contact you."

"Take your time," he answered. "Goodbye."

"Goodbye."

CHAPTER 27

LAST HAPPENINGS

CHAPTER 27
LAST HAPPENINGS

Marielena received a phone call from Commissioner Rivera several weeks after the trial. He asked her how she was and if she had thought any more about what she was going to do with the painting. Even though she was surprised to hear from him so soon, her response was, "I, personally, am doing well. I've been down in the village starting to do sketches again. I must have gotten some recognition as a local artist because of the trial and the Elliots hiring me to paint Margarita's portrait. Everyone seems so friendly and I already have several people who have purchased small paintings from me. I haven't decided what to do about the painting. I really appreciate your storing it for me."

He said, "I'm really glad things are going well for you. Please don't worry about the painting, our storeroom is quite large and there isn't any rush for you to remove it." He paused for a moment and then continued, "I was wondering if you would like to have a glass of wine down in the village at The Bellotto this evening with me?"

After thinking for a minute, she realized that she had not gone out of her attic apartment to do anything but work. At least, she was bringing in a little money now, but she hadn't thought about herself or her own personal life for weeks. She had nothing better to do this evening and Commissioner Rivera had been so kind to her before and during the trial. It would be nice to talk to him again. So, she answered, "I'd like that."

Commissioner Rivera asked, "If it's all right, I'll meet you there after I get off work at 8 o'clock?"

"I'll be there," she responded.

At 8 o'clock sharp they met and ordered their drinks. Their

conversation centered around some small talk about the day's activities, the weather, and the bar itself. Then Commissioner Rivera said to her, "I really would like it if you called me Diego. It's a bit awkward for both of us that you keep calling me Commissioner Rivera. I feel that we have become friends, rather than police commissioner and accused, don't you?"

As her eyes met his, she realized that he was making a real effort to be her friend. After all the publicity and lies that Charles had told about her, she needed a friend. It almost embarrassed her to think of him as a friend; but, in retrospect, he had always treated her kindly, listened to her, took her at her word, and had even asked her advice through the investigation and trial.

One glass of wine became two as they started talking about their lives. She was amazed that they had so many things in common. Without him saying it so much out loud, she realized that he was as lonely as she was.

Finally, he asked, "Would you allow me to take you to dinner now. I haven't eaten since breakfast and I'm hungry. Are you?"

She admitted, "Yes, I am."

Diego paid the bill and they left The Bellotto and went to the restaurant next door to eat. They discovered that they both loved croquettes, Mahon cheese, Caesar salads, and steak. When the meal was over, they walked through the village and stopped for another glass of wine at the bar closest to her apartment. They wished each other a pleasant evening and said goodnight.

Over the next few weeks, they meet for tapas, beer, wine, or dinner at least once or twice a week. As time passed, the villagers, while whispering about them, became used to seeing them as a pair. Señora Santiago laughed to herself as she heard Marielena singing softly to herself as she painted up in her room. Although she felt that the time might come when she would have to look for a new boarder, the señora was happy to see Marielena seem so happy. She had grown to love her boarder and wished the best for her.

One evening as they were eating dinner together and the meal had concluded, Diego handed Marielena an official-looking envelope. The return address on the envelope was The Prado Art Museum in Madrid. Marielena asked, "What is this?"

Diego answered, "It's something which I've been working on for a while." He watched her as she opened the envelope and started to read the enclosed letter.

"This can't be true," she said.

"Oh, it is. The painting, which is now in the jail's storeroom and which belongs to you, is being purchased by the museum to be included in their permanent collection. Because Margarita was Miss Santandar, Miss Palma, Miss Bealaric Islands, Miss Spain, and Miss World, the Spanish government sees her as a historical and important figure to the Spanish people. 'The Spanish Beauty' is going to be in the Prado for all Spaniards to revere, thanks to you."

"But the amount they're willing to pay for it is way more than what Charles Elliot owed for the entire painting," stated Marielena. "And they're going to pay to have it framed, shipped, and celebrated in a grand opening exhibit."

"That's right," he answered.

She replied in a hushed voice, "I can't believe it."

"Well, it's true. You will now have a major painting in the Prado, one of Spain's major art museums, in fact one of the major art museums of the world."

"I still can't believe it."

"I doubt you will ever have to worry about commissions and fine art galleries wanting to hang your work in the future."

"Oh," she said, beaming at him. "How did you manage this?"

"Well, you recall that I told you that I had been a policeman in Madrid. When I was there, I met a number of people at the museum when they had several paintings stolen. I recovered those paintings and they were returned to the museum. I have remained in contact with a couple of the curators there who were very grateful to have the paintings recovered. I just called them, explaining the circumstances of the painting of Margarita. They were intrigued and asked that I send them a photograph of the painting, which I did. They were so impressed that a museum representative came down from Madrid and looked at the painting this last week. I kept it a secret from you because I didn't want you to get your hopes up and maybe become disappointed if nothing came of it. Now, I'm so happy that I did it because you'll be a famous artist now."

With tears in her eyes, she jumped up, ran around the table, and kissed him.

"Oh, you dear man!" She exclaimed.

EPILOGUE

EPILOGUE

Diego took Marielena's hand as they walked together through the village. He couldn't believe his good fortune. She really loved him. Her every look at him confirmed it. How could he have questioned her relationship with Charles Elliot? How had he jumped to conclusions based only on circumstantial evidence? He had always prided himself on being a better policeman than to look at just the outside of things. Marielena was an absolute wonder. She had always been innocent. Her only failing was in accepting a commission which she had thought would help her financially. Then, she had almost single-handedly solved the murder herself. She had looked for and found evidence and had kept evidence for Margarita which had helped convict Charles of Margarita's murder.

Laughing out loud, he said to her, "Marielena, I know you're a fantastic artist, but I have two jobs in line for you if you want them."

Looking up at him, she asked, "What are they?"

He answered her, "Besides being a good artist, you're also a good detective. The police department right now needs one. We have decided to hire a part-time detective to fill that new vacancy. So - how about working part time, when you're not painting, for the police department?"

She nodded silently, and said, "I think I'd like that. But, what's the second job?"

Diego grinned broadly and, sinking down onto one knee, asked, "Will you marry me and take on the job of being the police commissioner's wife?"

She answered, "I thought you'd never ask me. Yes - a thousand times - yes!"

ABOUT THE AUTHOR ELAINE C. WOLFE

Retired educator and artist, Dr. Elaine Wolfe, had on her bucket list the desire to write a novel. Her preliminary notes for The Spanish Beauty began five years ago on one of her visits to see her daughter who lives in Mallorca, Spain; but the writing was accomplished during the quarantine for the Covid-19 pandemic. Dr. Wolfe combines her story-telling abilities developed during 36 years of teaching biology, with her lifetime experiences as a professional artist, and her love of Spanish culture.

Dr. Wolfe has traveled to every continent except Antarctica, has been recognized nationally for her teaching abilities, and has been recognized as an award-winning professional artist. She has been, for forty years, and continues to be an artist-owner of the CCA Art Gallery in Carmel, IN.

Dr. Wolfe is a published author of her 400-page dissertation, science articles in "The American Biology Teacher" and "The Hoosier Science Teacher", and poems in The National Library of Poetry's "Best Poems of 1998" and "Whispers at Dusk". She is a Distinguished Purdue University Alumna in the School of Science.

www.ingramcontent.com/pod-product-compliance
Lightning Source LLC
Chambersburg PA
CBHW071543110726
47908CB00007B/1974

* 9 7 8 1 7 3 3 9 6 1 7 4 5 *